WITHDRAWN

D1247409

STONE ARCH BOOKS
a capstone imprint

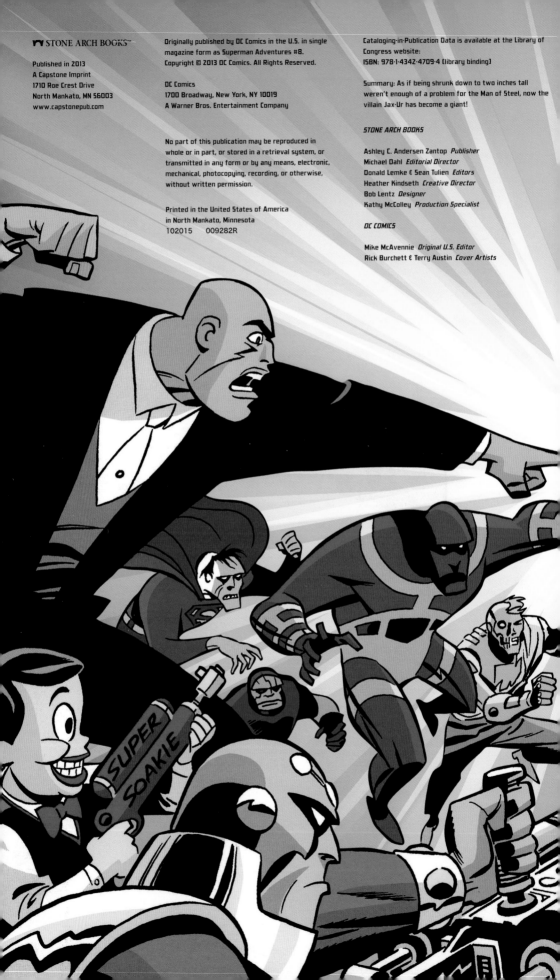

STONE ARCH BOOKS™

Published in 2013
A Capstone Imprint
1710 Roe Crest Drive
North Mankato, MN 56003
www.capstonepub.com

Originally published by DC Comics in the U.S. in single magazine form as Superman Adventures #8.

DC Comics
1700 Broadway, New York, NY 10019
A Warner Bros. Entertainment Company

Printed in the United States of America
in North Mankato, Minnesota
102015 009282R

Cataloging-in-Publication Data is available at the Library of Congress website:
ISBN: 978-1-4342-4709-4 (library binding)

Summary: As if being shrunk down to two inches tall weren't enough of a problem for the Man of Steel, now the villain Jax-Ur has become a giant!

STONE ARCH BOOKS

Ashley C. Andersen Zantop *Publisher*
Michael Dahl *Editorial Director*
Donald Lemke & Sean Tulien *Editors*
Heather Kindseth *Creative Director*
Bob Lentz *Designer*
Kathy McColley *Production Specialist*

DC COMICS

Mike McAvennie *Original U.S. Editor*
Rick Burchett & Terry Austin *Cover Artists*

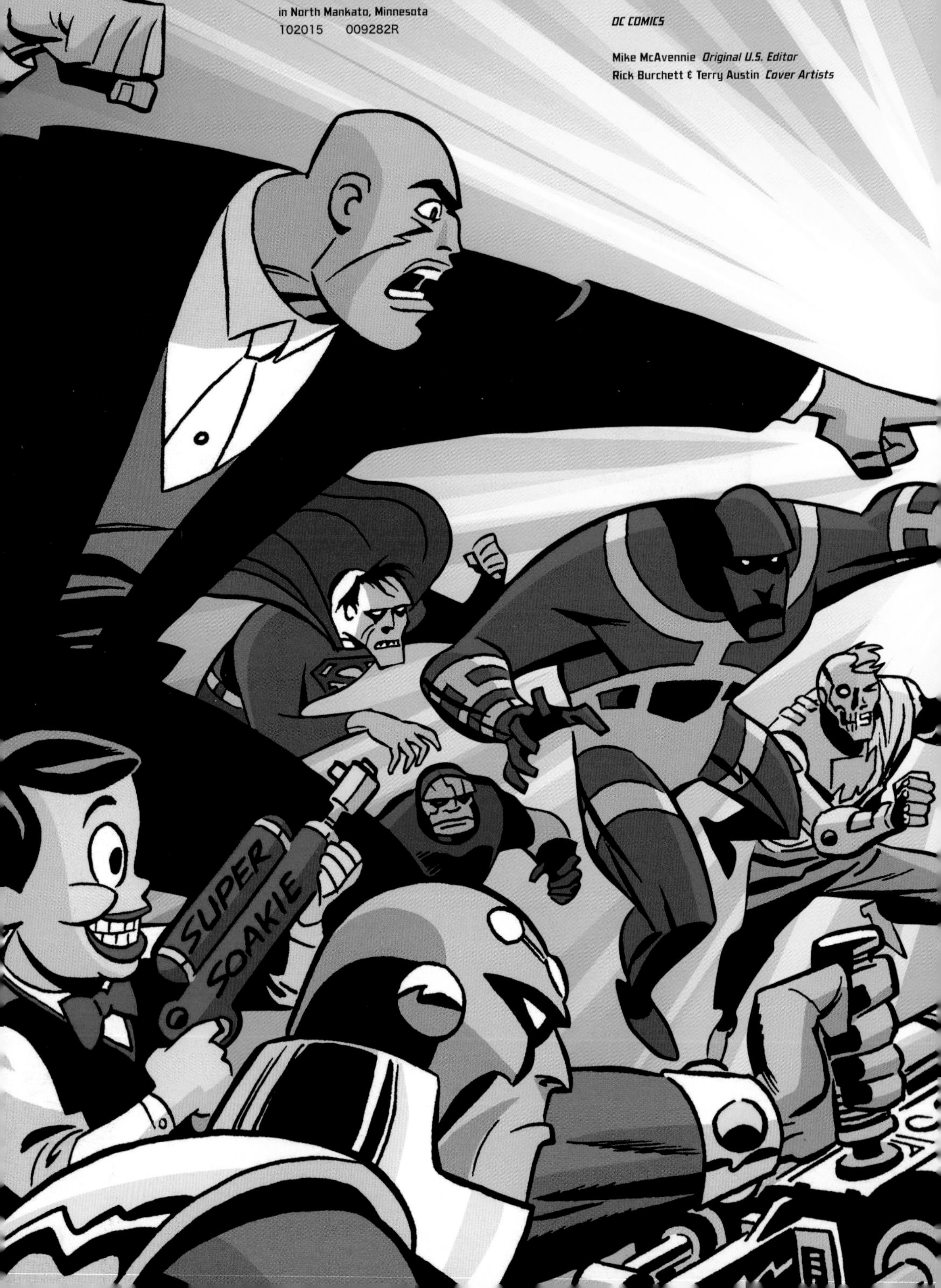
SUPER SOAKIE

SUPERMAN ADVENTURES

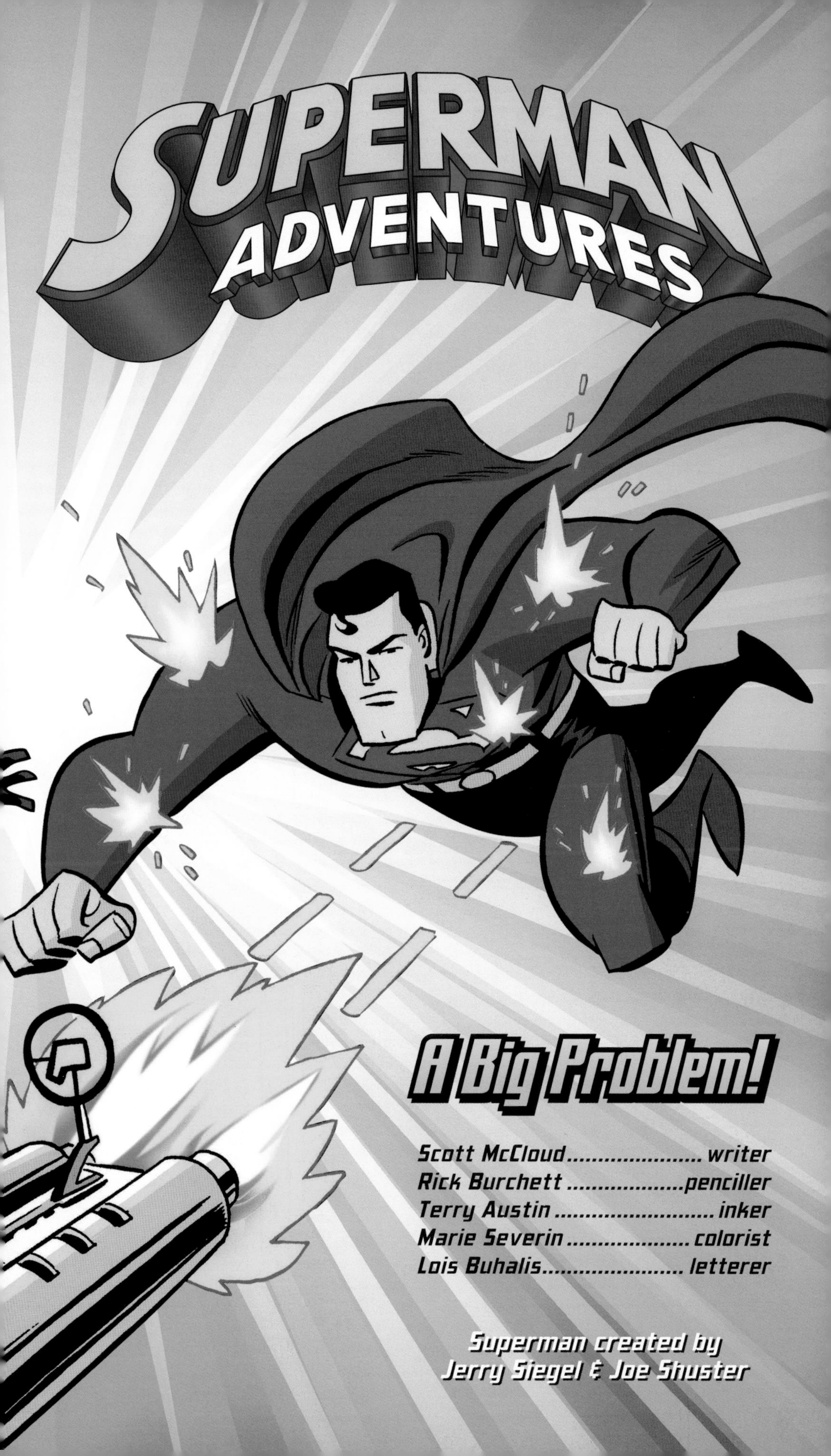

A Big Problem!

Scott McCloud........................ writer
Rick Burchett ....penciller
Terry Austin .... inker
Marie Severin .... colorist
Lois Buhalis......................... letterer

Superman created by
Jerry Siegel & Joe Shuster

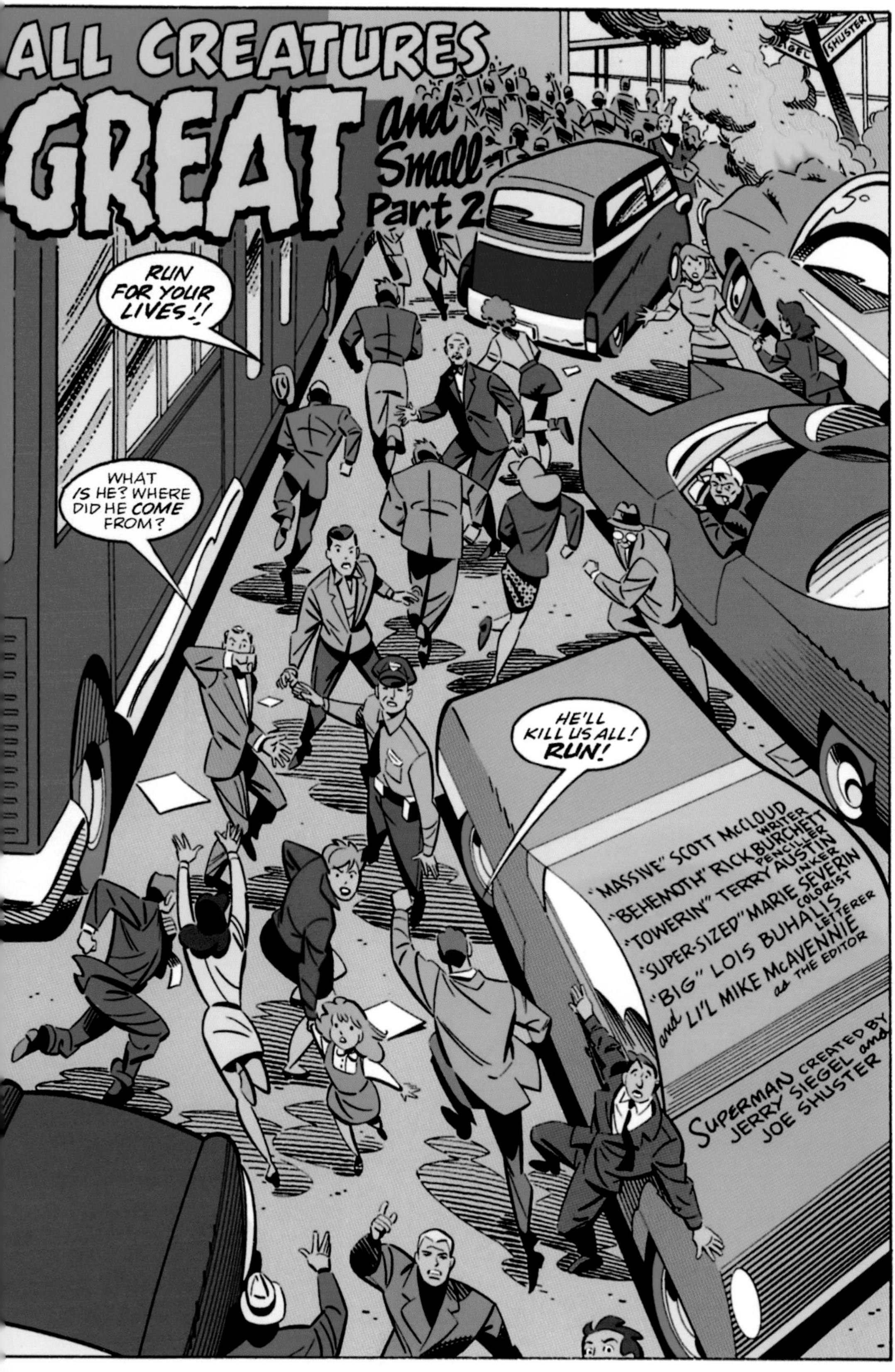

ALL CREATURES
GREAT
and Small
Part 2
SIEGEL
SHUSTER
RUN FOR YOUR LIVES!!
WHAT IS HE? WHERE DID HE COME FROM?
HE'LL KILL US ALL! RUN!
"MASSIVE" SCOTT McCLOUD WRITER
"BEHEMOTH" RICK BURCHETT PENCILLER
"TOWERIN" TERRY AUSTIN INKER
"SUPER-SIZED" MARIE SEVERIN COLORIST
"BIG" LOIS BUHALIS LETTERER
and LI'L MIKE McAVENNIE as THE EDITOR
SUPERMAN CREATED BY JERRY SIEGEL and JOE SHUSTER

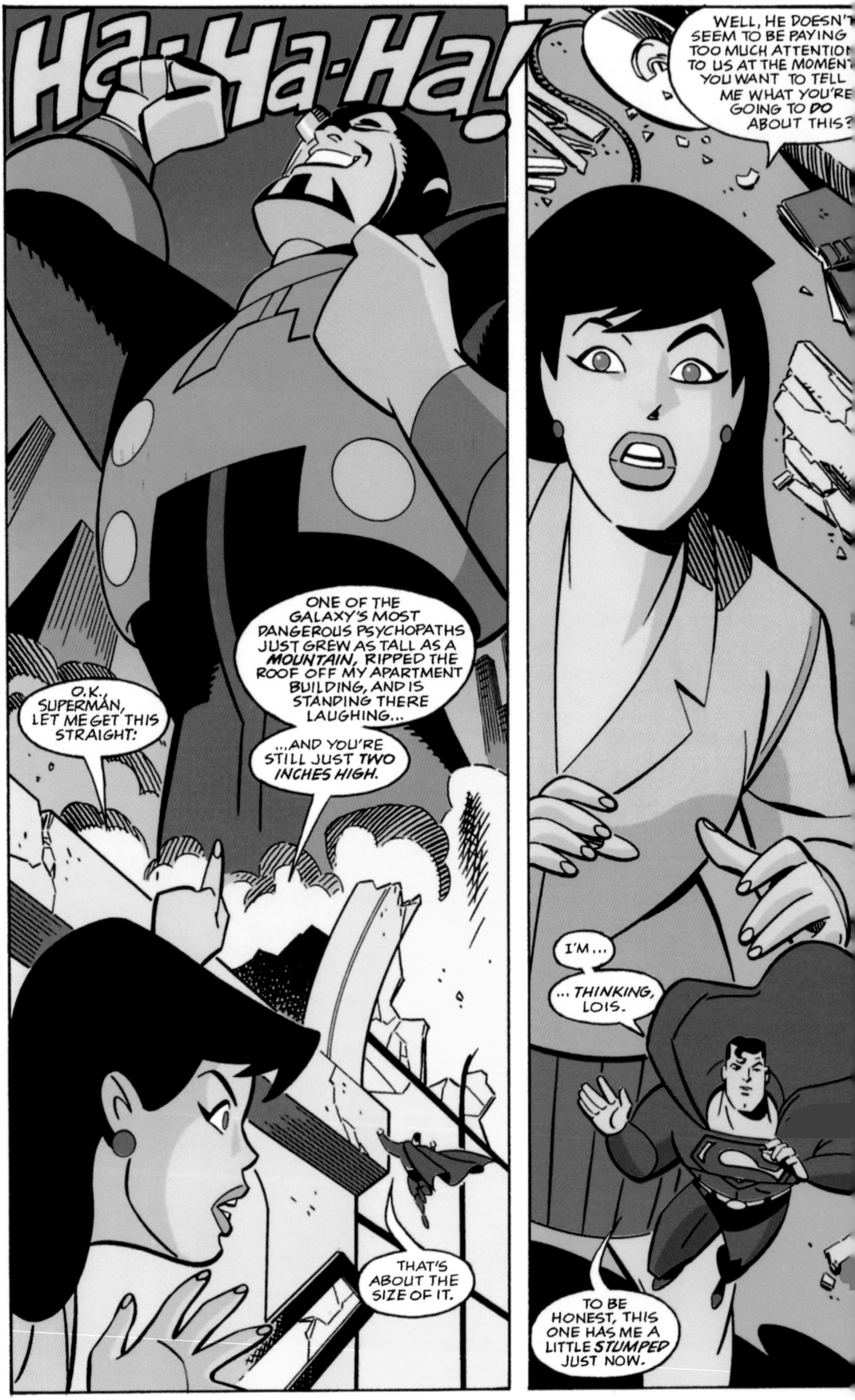

HA-HA-HA-HA!
O.K., SUPERMAN, LET ME GET THIS STRAIGHT:
ONE OF THE GALAXY'S MOST DANGEROUS PSYCHOPATHS JUST GREW AS TALL AS A MOUNTAIN, RIPPED THE ROOF OFF MY APARTMENT BUILDING, AND IS STANDING THERE LAUGHING...
...AND YOU'RE STILL JUST TWO INCHES HIGH.
THAT'S ABOUT THE SIZE OF IT.
WELL, HE DOESN'T SEEM TO BE PAYING TOO MUCH ATTENTION TO US AT THE MOMENT. YOU WANT TO TELL ME WHAT YOU'RE GOING TO DO ABOUT THIS?
I'M...
...THINKING, LOIS.
TO BE HONEST, THIS ONE HAS ME A LITTLE STUMPED JUST NOW.

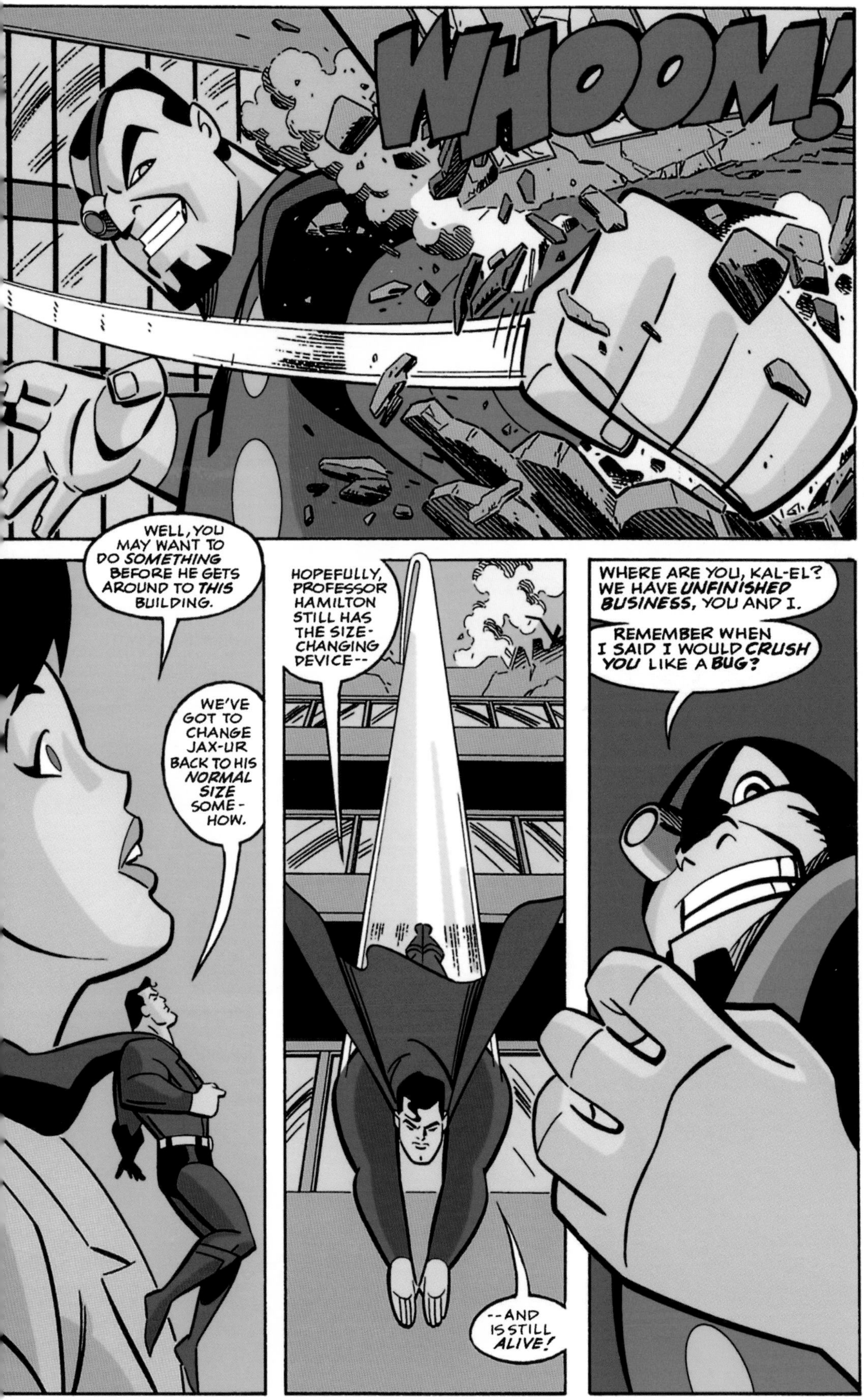
WHOOM!
WELL, YOU MAY WANT TO DO SOMETHING BEFORE HE GETS AROUND TO THIS BUILDING.
WE'VE GOT TO CHANGE JAX-UR BACK TO HIS NORMAL SIZE SOME-HOW.
HOPEFULLY, PROFESSOR HAMILTON STILL HAS THE SIZE-CHANGING DEVICE--
--AND IS STILL ALIVE!
WHERE ARE YOU, KAL-EL? WE HAVE UNFINISHED BUSINESS, YOU AND I.
REMEMBER WHEN I SAID I WOULD CRUSH YOU LIKE A BUG?

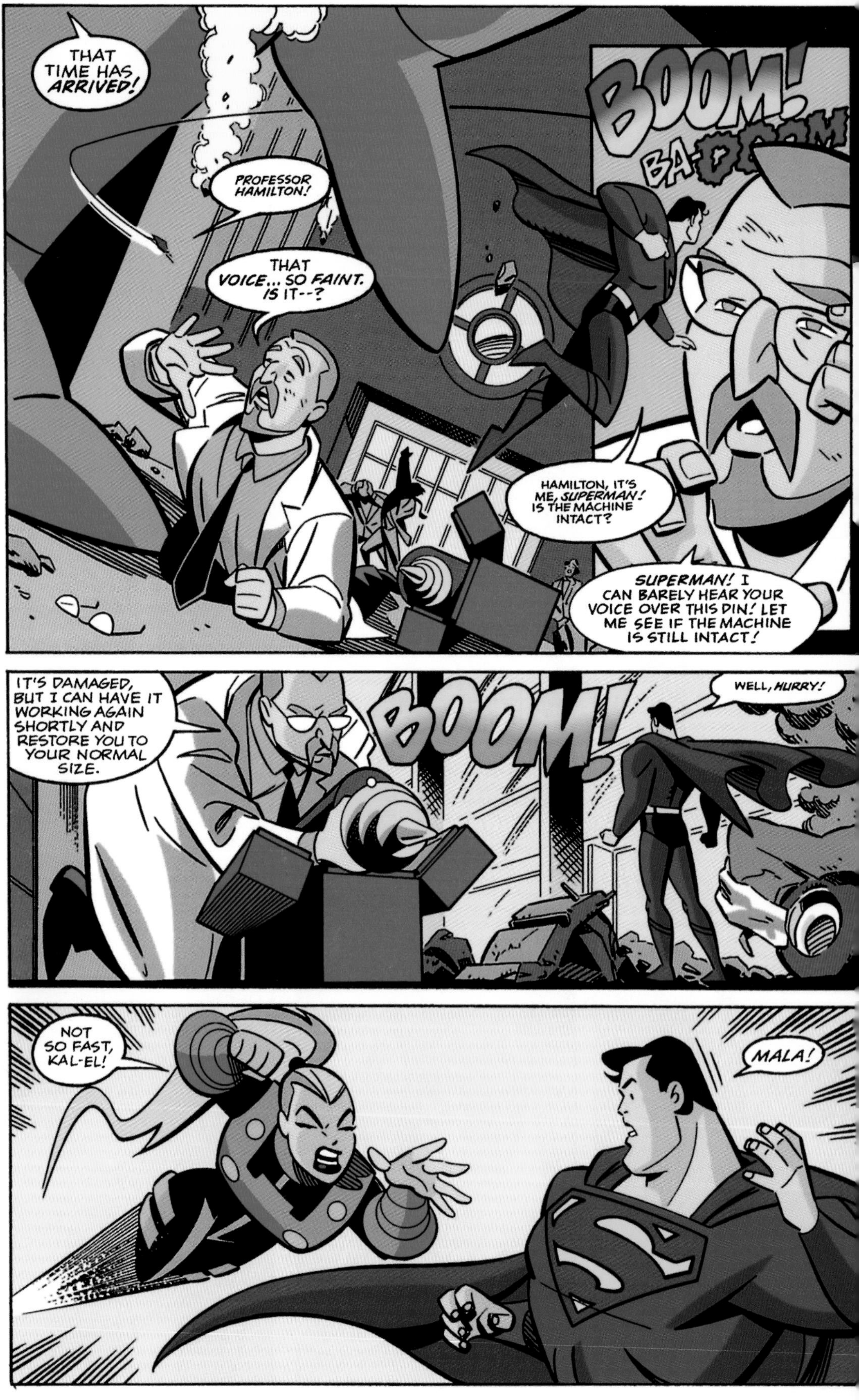
THAT TIME HAS ARRIVED!
PROFESSOR HAMILTON!
THAT VOICE... SO FAINT. IS IT--?
BOOM! BA-DOOM
HAMILTON, IT'S ME, SUPERMAN! IS THE MACHINE INTACT?
SUPERMAN! I CAN BARELY HEAR YOUR VOICE OVER THIS DIN! LET ME SEE IF THE MACHINE IS STILL INTACT!
IT'S DAMAGED, BUT I CAN HAVE IT WORKING AGAIN SHORTLY AND RESTORE YOU TO YOUR NORMAL SIZE.
BOOM!
WELL, HURRY!
NOT SO FAST, KAL-EL!
MALA!

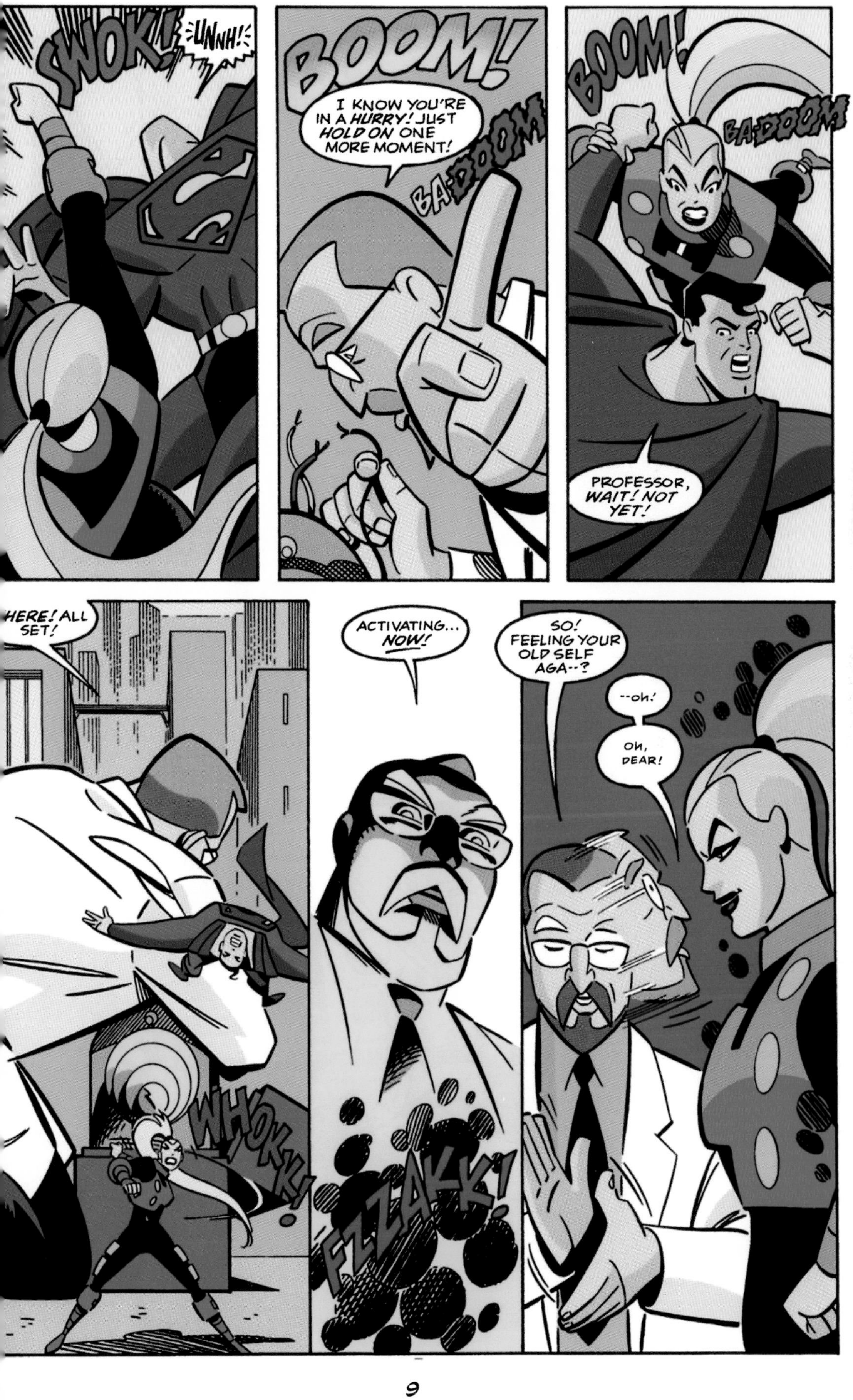
SWOK!
UNNH!
BOOM!
I KNOW YOU'RE IN A HURRY! JUST HOLD ON ONE MORE MOMENT!
BA-DOOM
BOOM!
BA-DOOM
PROFESSOR, WAIT! NOT YET!
HERE! ALL SET!
WHOKK!
ACTIVATING... NOW!
FZZAKK!
SO! FEELING YOUR OLD SELF AGA--?
--oh!
Oh, DEAR!

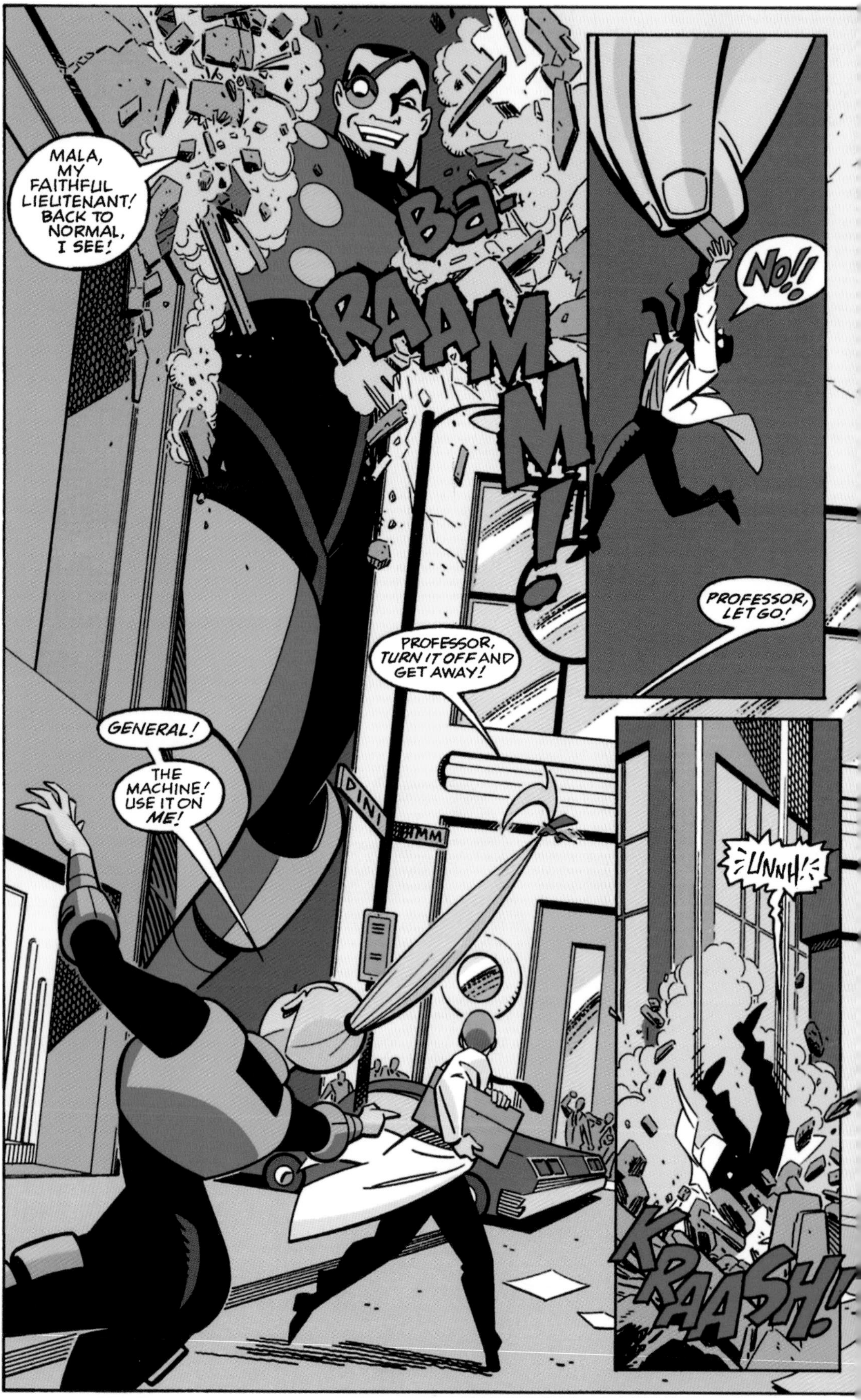
MALA, MY FAITHFUL LIEUTENANT! BACK TO NORMAL, I SEE!
BA-RAAMM!
NO!!
PROFESSOR, LET GO!
PROFESSOR, TURN IT OFF AND GET AWAY!
GENERAL!
THE MACHINE! USE IT ON ME!
DINI
UNNH!
KRAASH!

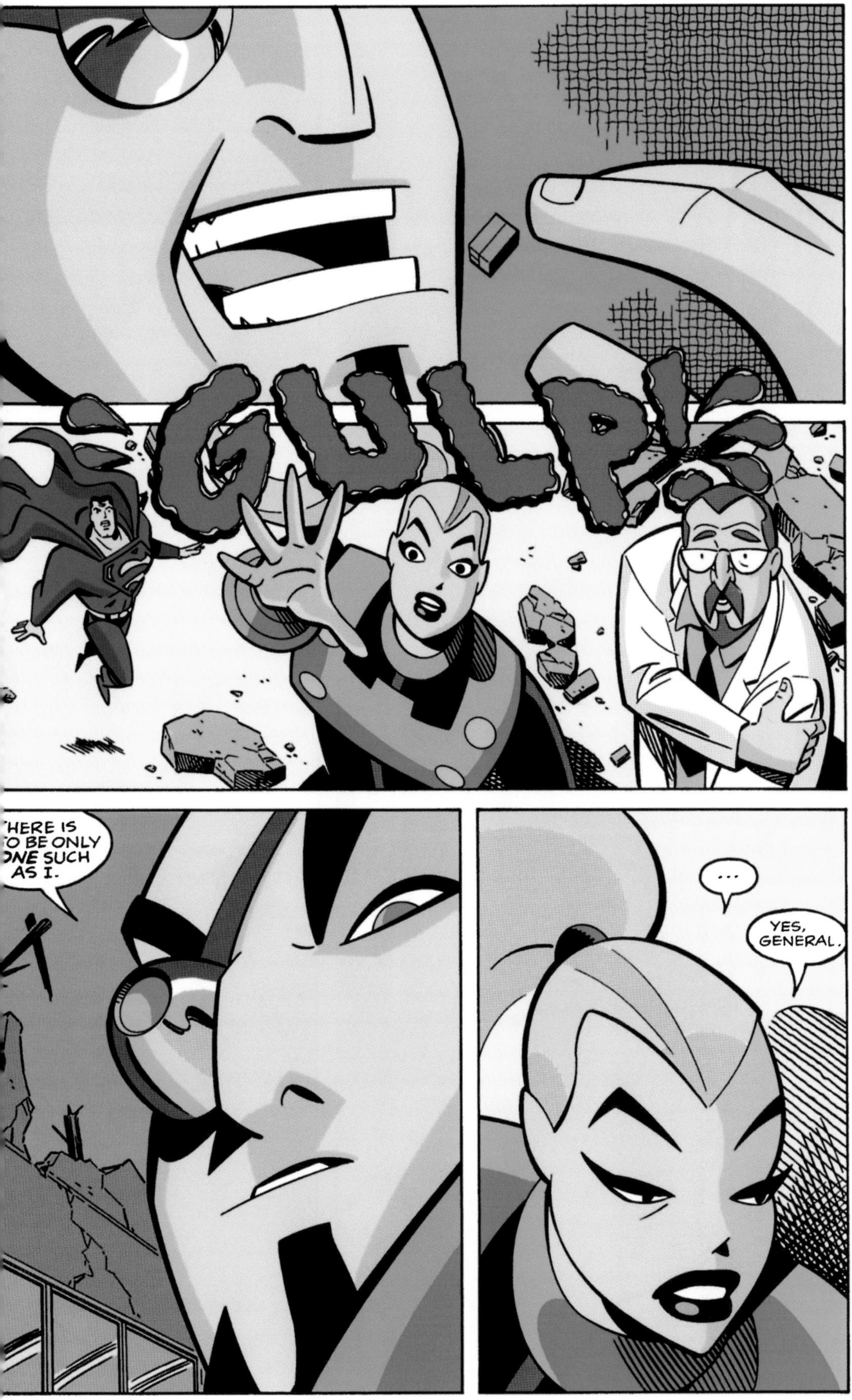
GULP!
THERE IS TO BE ONLY ONE SUCH AS I.
...
YES, GENERAL.

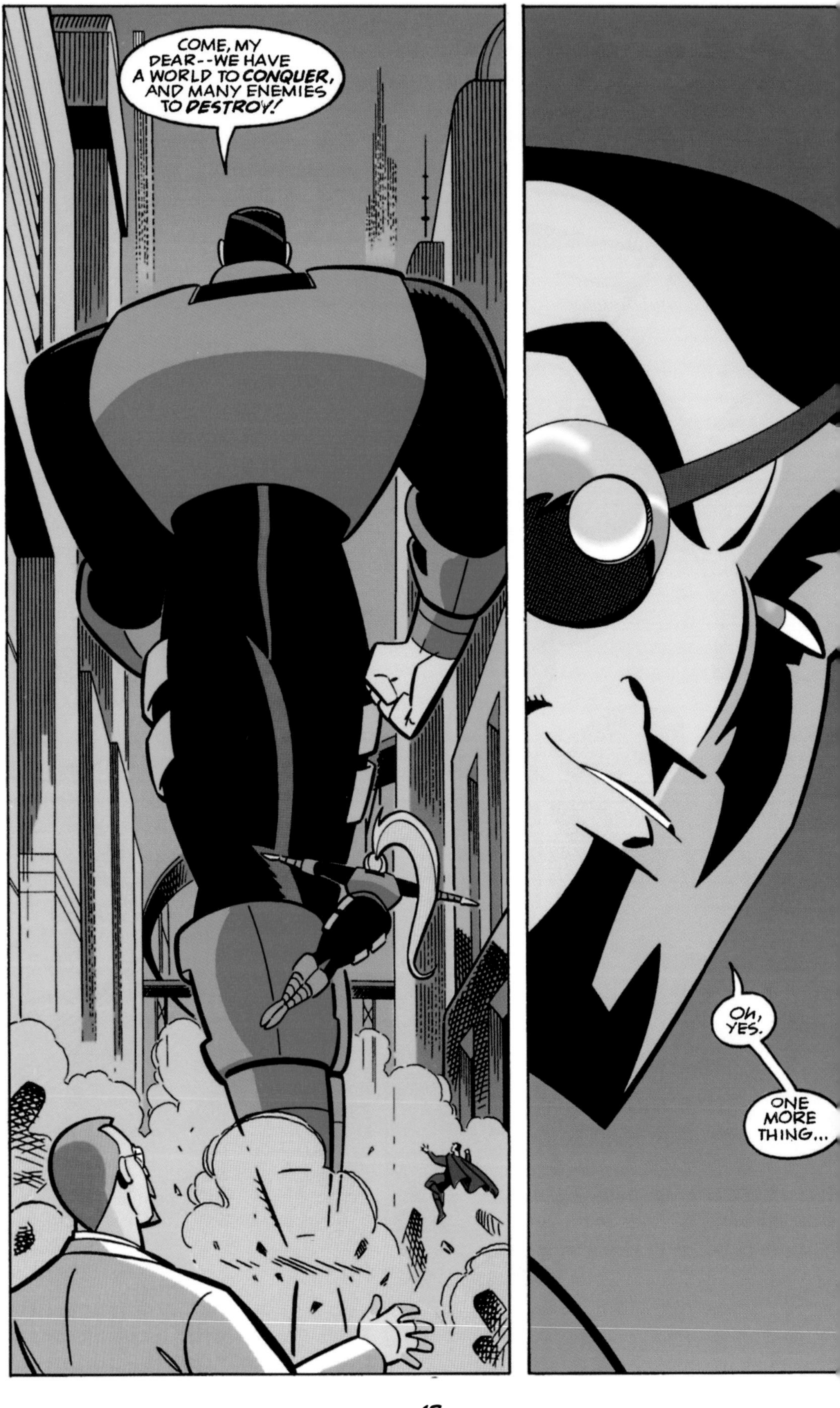
COME, MY DEAR--WE HAVE A WORLD TO CONQUER, AND MANY ENEMIES TO DESTROY!
Oh, YES.
ONE MORE THING...

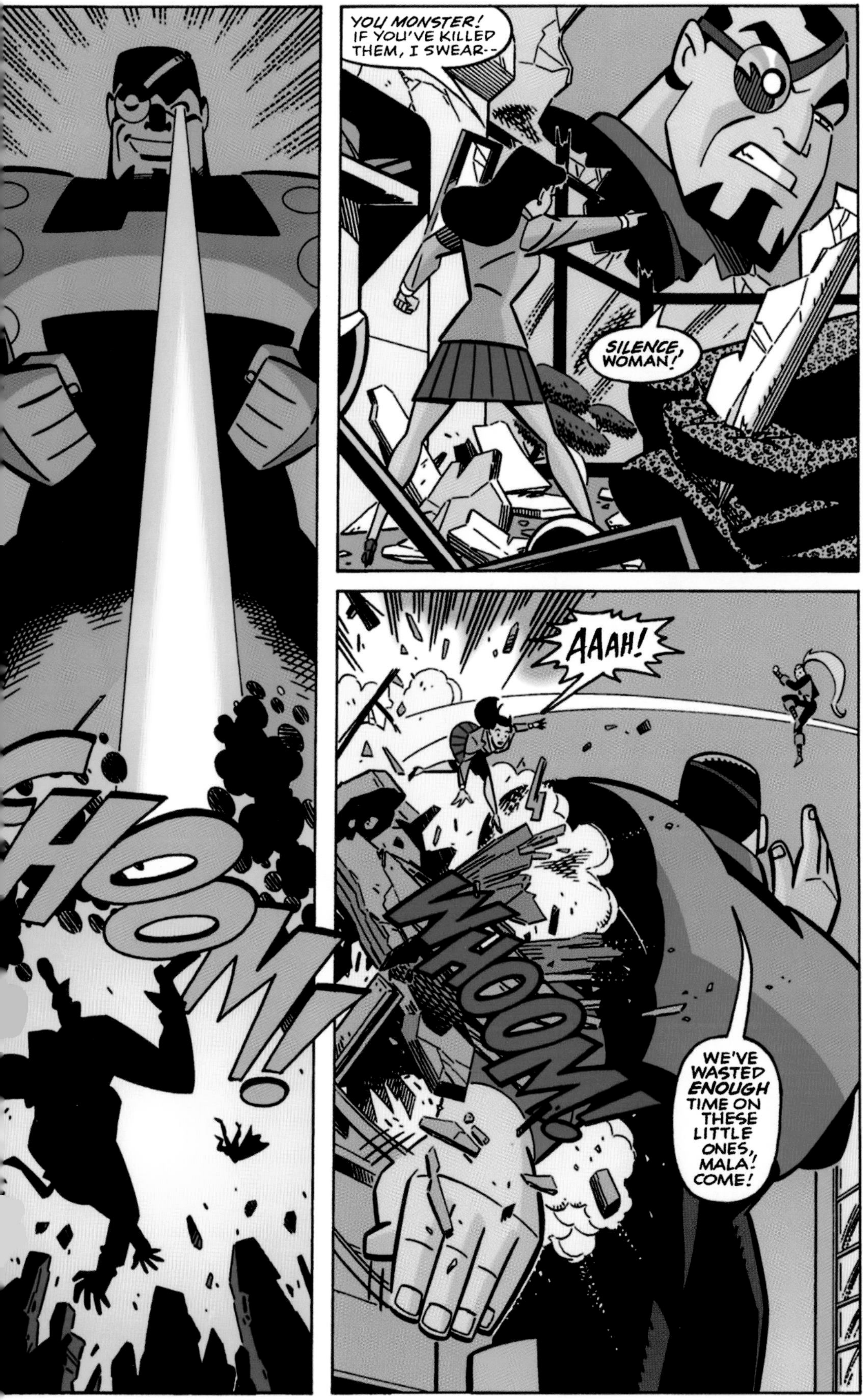
WHOOM!
YOU MONSTER! IF YOU'VE KILLED THEM, I SWEAR--
SILENCE, WOMAN!
AAAH!
WHOOM!
WE'VE WASTED ENOUGH TIME ON THESE LITTLE ONES, MALA! COME!

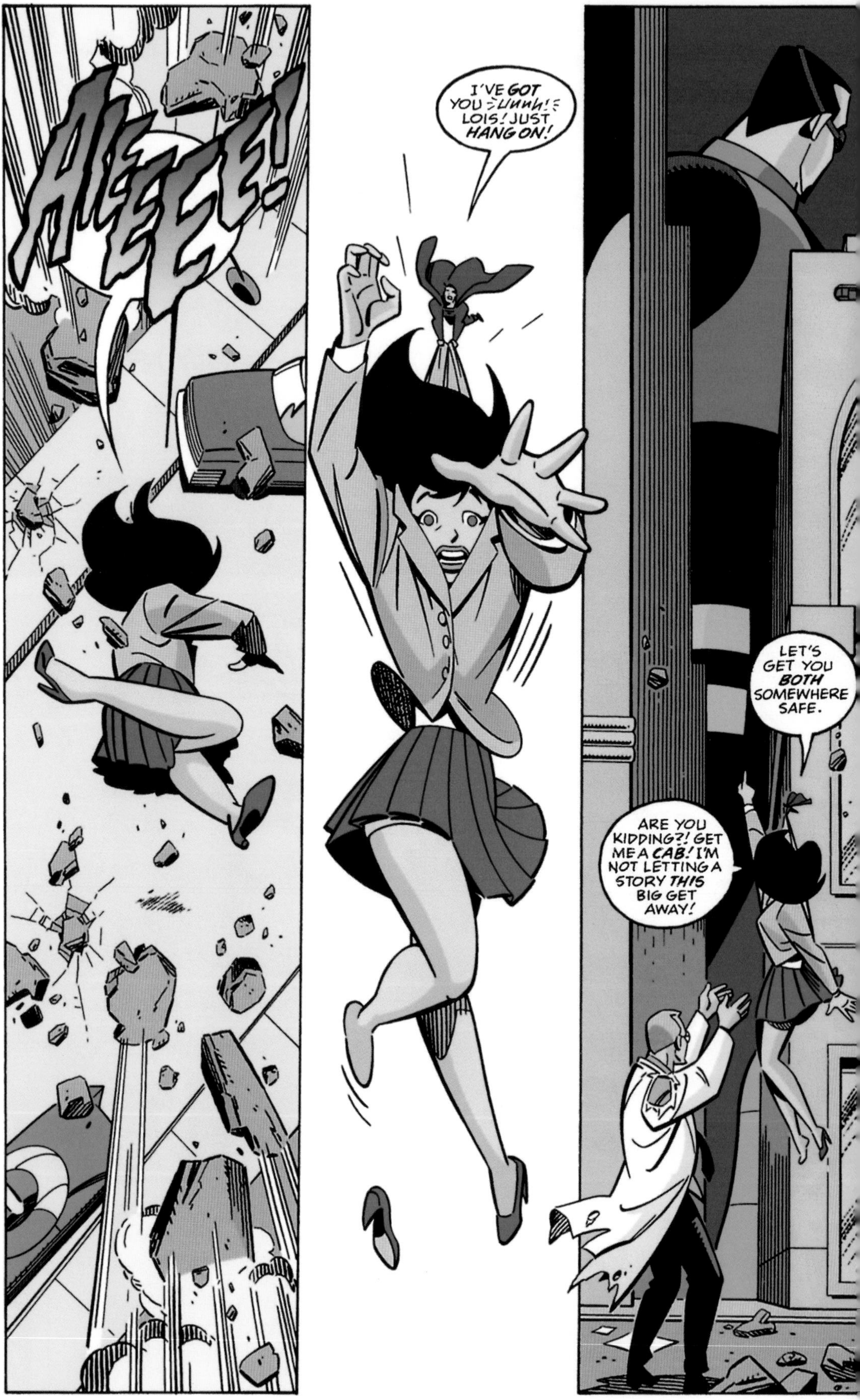
AIEEEE!
I'VE GOT YOU =UNNH!= LOIS! JUST HANG ON!
LET'S GET YOU BOTH SOMEWHERE SAFE.
ARE YOU KIDDING?! GET ME A CAB! I'M NOT LETTING A STORY THIS BIG GET AWAY!

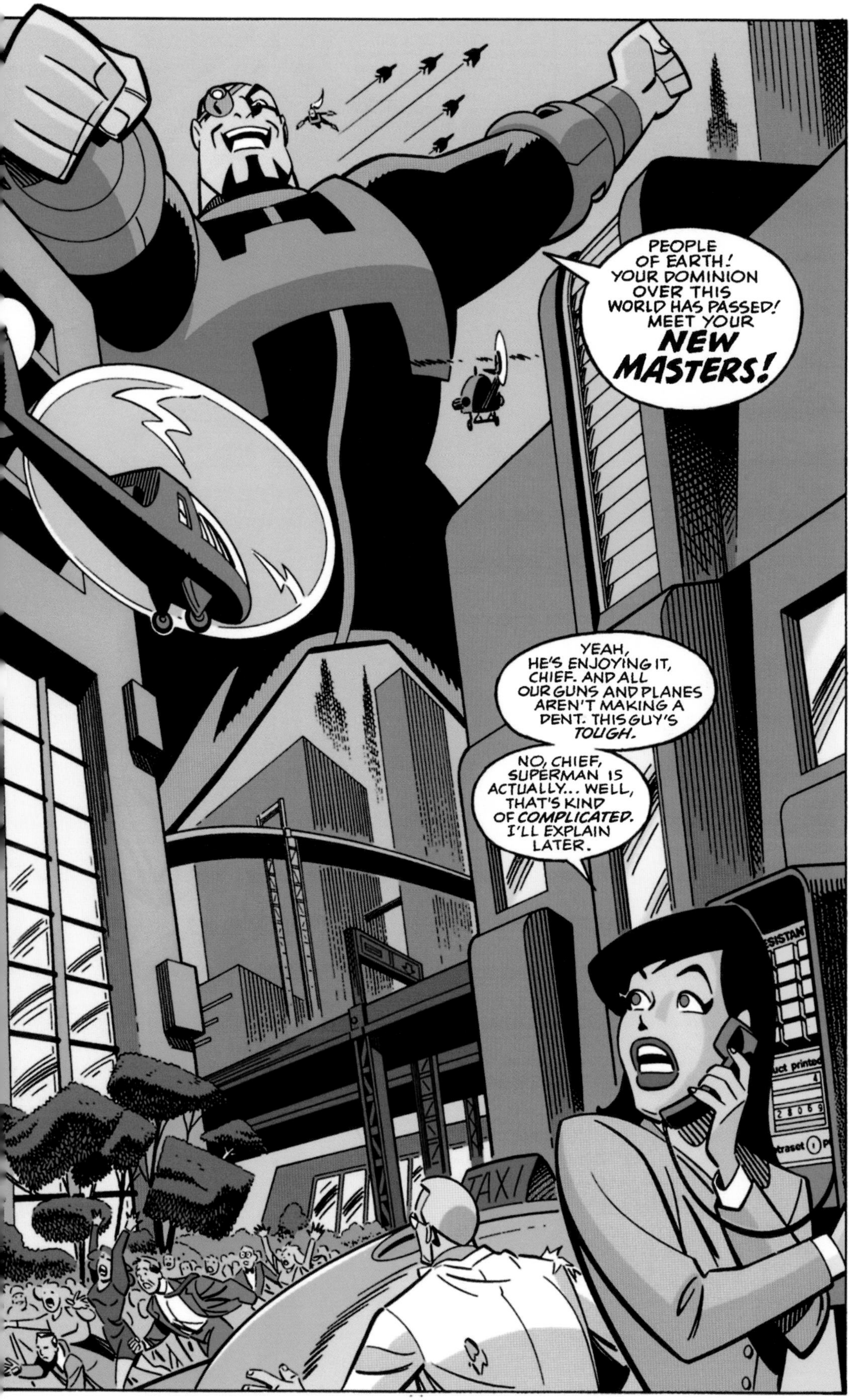
PEOPLE OF EARTH! YOUR DOMINION OVER THIS WORLD HAS PASSED! MEET YOUR **NEW MASTERS!**
YEAH, HE'S ENJOYING IT, CHIEF. AND ALL OUR GUNS AND PLANES AREN'T MAKING A DENT. THIS GUY'S *TOUGH.*
NO, CHIEF, SUPERMAN IS ACTUALLY... WELL, THAT'S KIND OF *COMPLICATED.* I'LL EXPLAIN LATER.
TAXI

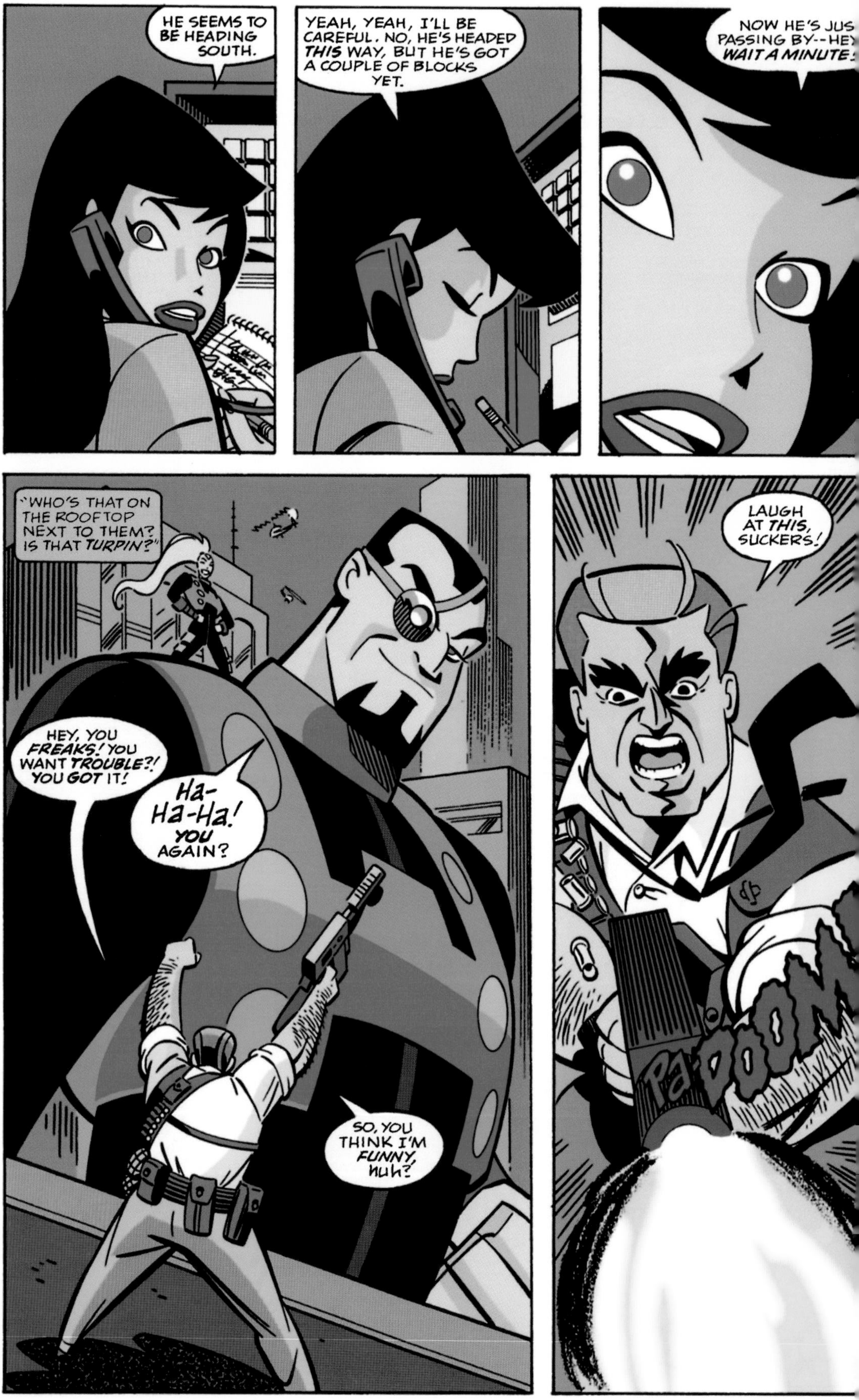
HE SEEMS TO BE HEADING SOUTH.
YEAH, YEAH, I'LL BE CAREFUL. NO, HE'S HEADED THIS WAY, BUT HE'S GOT A COUPLE OF BLOCKS YET.
NOW HE'S JUS PASSING BY--HEY WAIT A MINUTE!
"WHO'S THAT ON THE ROOFTOP NEXT TO THEM? IS THAT TURPIN?"
HEY, YOU FREAKS! YOU WANT TROUBLE?! YOU GOT IT!
Ha-Ha-Ha! YOU AGAIN?
SO, YOU THINK I'M FUNNY, huh?
LAUGH AT THIS, SUCKERS!
Pa-DOOM

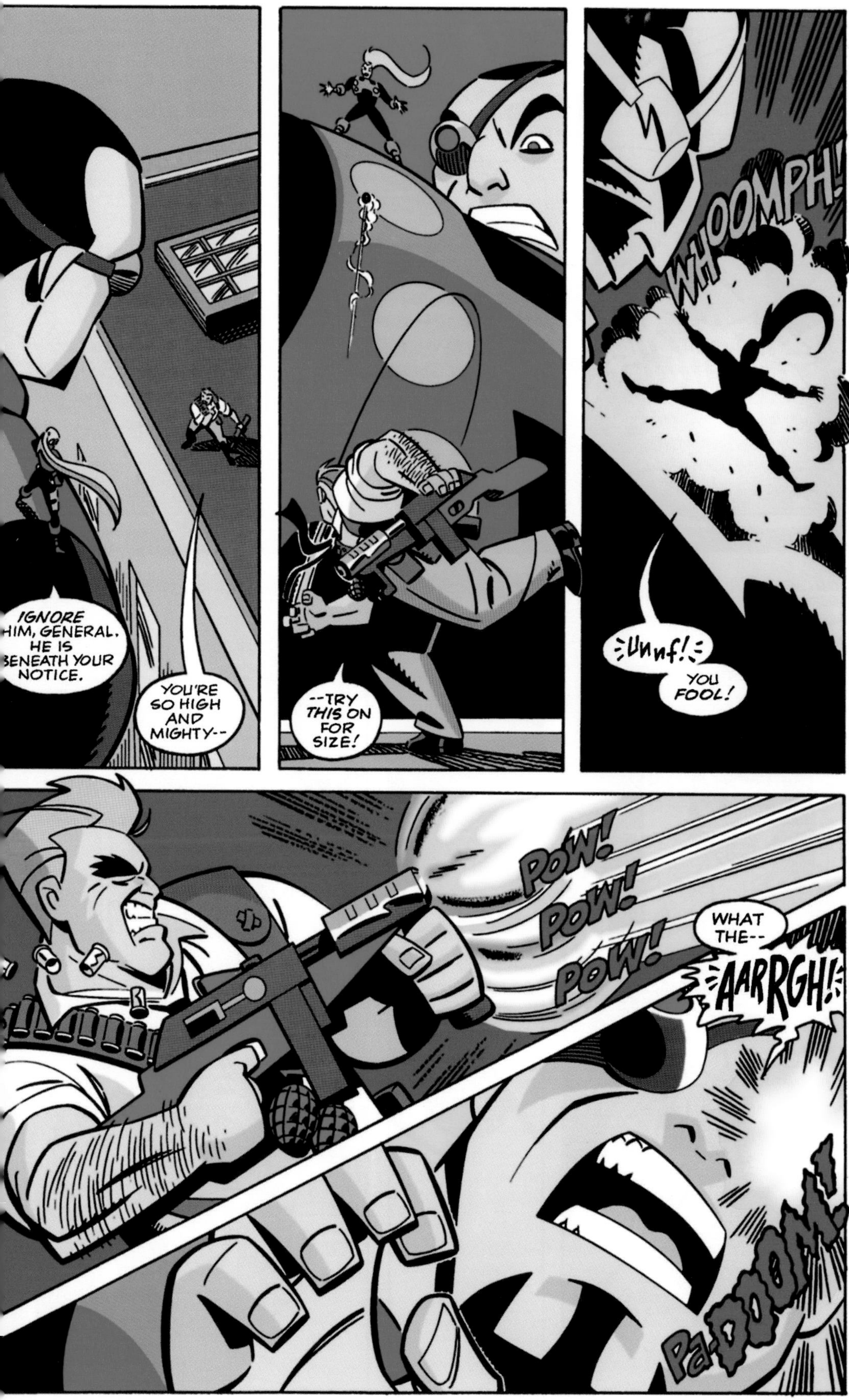
IGNORE HIM, GENERAL. HE IS BENEATH YOUR NOTICE.
YOU'RE SO HIGH AND MIGHTY--
--TRY THIS ON FOR SIZE!
WHOOMPH!
Unnf!
YOU FOOL!
POW!
POW!
POW!
WHAT THE--
AARRGH!
Pa-DOOM!

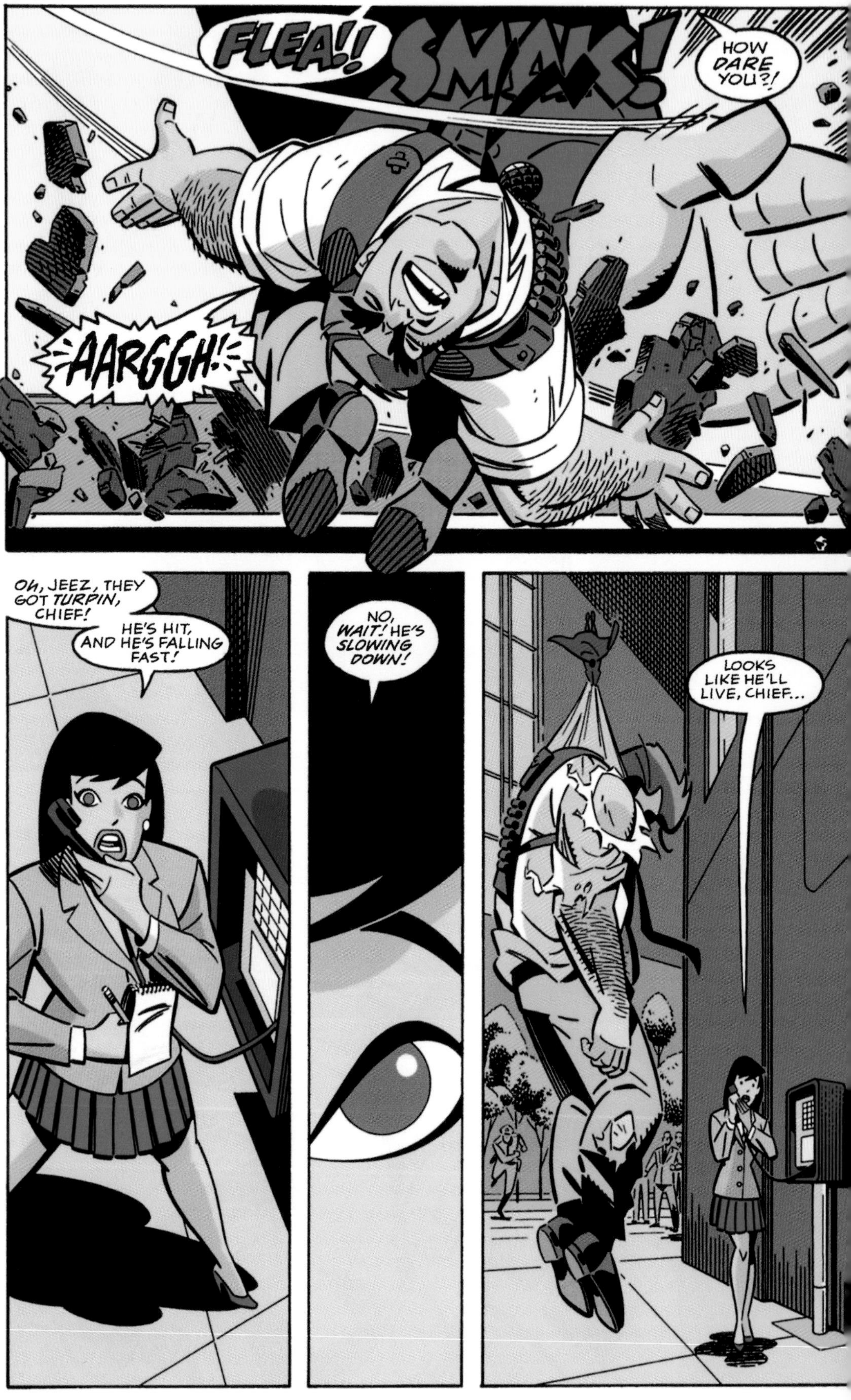
FLEA!!
SMAK!
HOW DARE YOU?!
AARGGH!
OH, JEEZ, THEY GOT TURPIN, CHIEF!
HE'S HIT, AND HE'S FALLING FAST!
NO, WAIT! HE'S SLOWING DOWN!
LOOKS LIKE HE'LL LIVE, CHIEF...

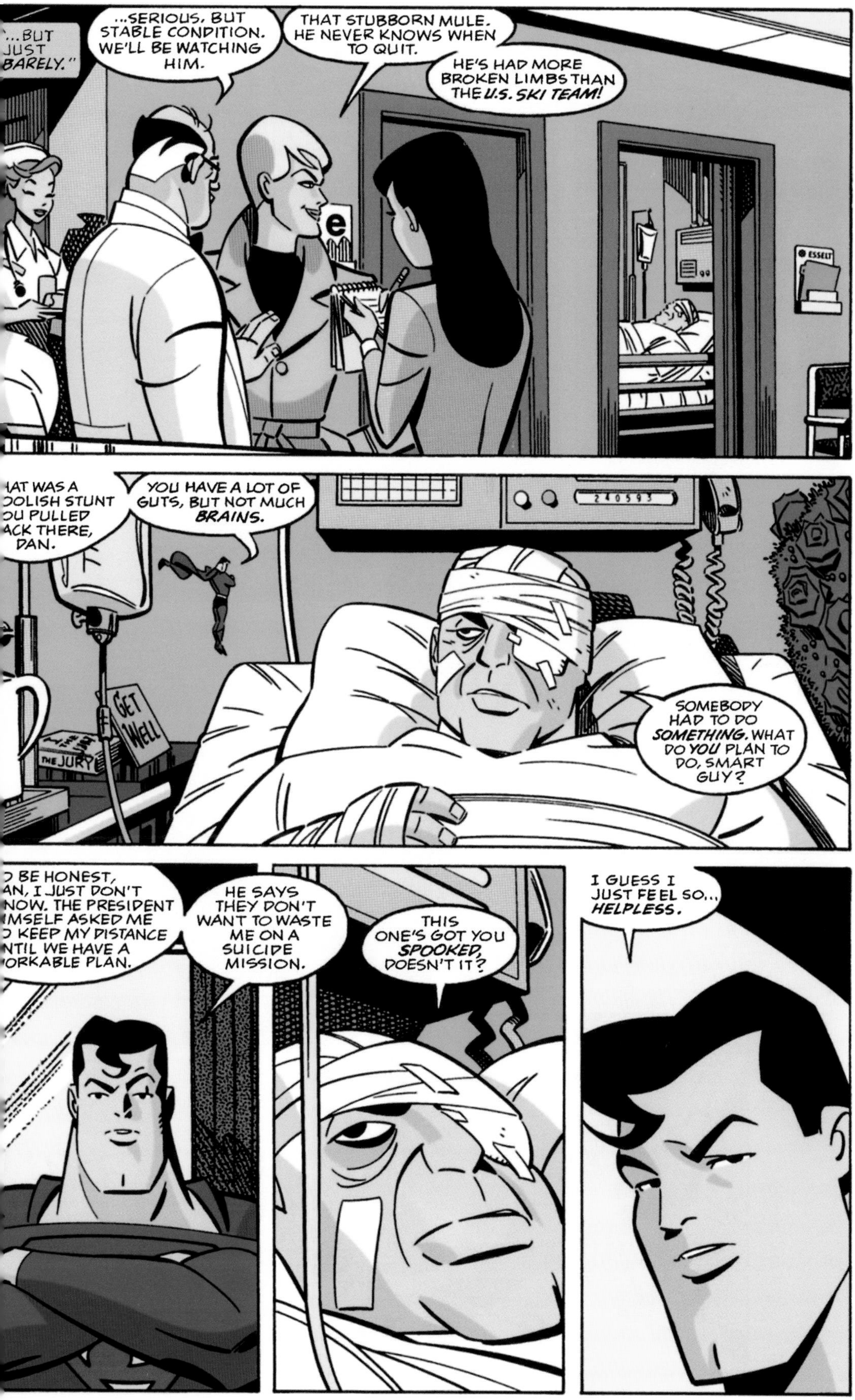
"...BUT JUST BARELY."
...SERIOUS, BUT STABLE CONDITION. WE'LL BE WATCHING HIM.
THAT STUBBORN MULE. HE NEVER KNOWS WHEN TO QUIT.
HE'S HAD MORE BROKEN LIMBS THAN THE U.S. SKI TEAM!
HAT WAS A OOLISH STUNT OU PULLED ACK THERE, DAN.
YOU HAVE A LOT OF GUTS, BUT NOT MUCH BRAINS.
GET WELL
THE JURY
SOMEBODY HAD TO DO SOMETHING. WHAT DO YOU PLAN TO DO, SMART GUY?
O BE HONEST, AN, I JUST DON'T NOW. THE PRESIDENT IMSELF ASKED ME O KEEP MY DISTANCE NTIL WE HAVE A ORKABLE PLAN.
HE SAYS THEY DON'T WANT TO WASTE ME ON A SUICIDE MISSION.
THIS ONE'S GOT YOU SPOOKED, DOESN'T IT?
I GUESS I JUST FEEL SO... HELPLESS.

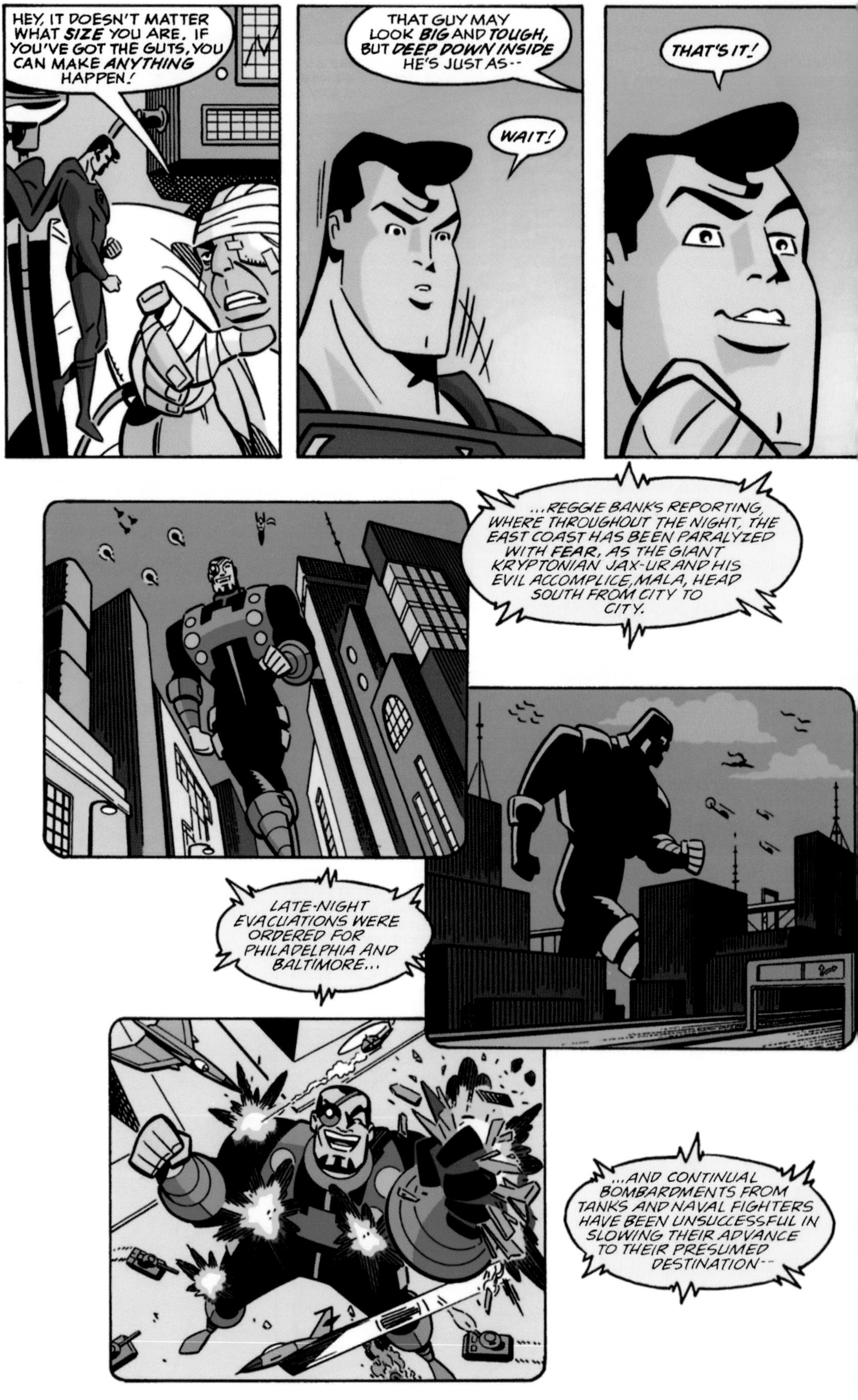
HEY, IT DOESN'T MATTER WHAT SIZE YOU ARE. IF YOU'VE GOT THE GUTS, YOU CAN MAKE ANYTHING HAPPEN!
THAT GUY MAY LOOK BIG AND TOUGH, BUT DEEP DOWN INSIDE HE'S JUST AS--
WAIT!
THAT'S IT!
...REGGIE BANKS REPORTING, WHERE THROUGHOUT THE NIGHT, THE EAST COAST HAS BEEN PARALYZED WITH FEAR, AS THE GIANT KRYPTONIAN JAX-UR AND HIS EVIL ACCOMPLICE, MALA, HEAD SOUTH FROM CITY TO CITY.
LATE-NIGHT EVACUATIONS WERE ORDERED FOR PHILADELPHIA AND BALTIMORE...
...AND CONTINUAL BOMBARDMENTS FROM TANKS AND NAVAL FIGHTERS HAVE BEEN UNSUCCESSFUL IN SLOWING THEIR ADVANCE TO THEIR PRESUMED DESTINATION--

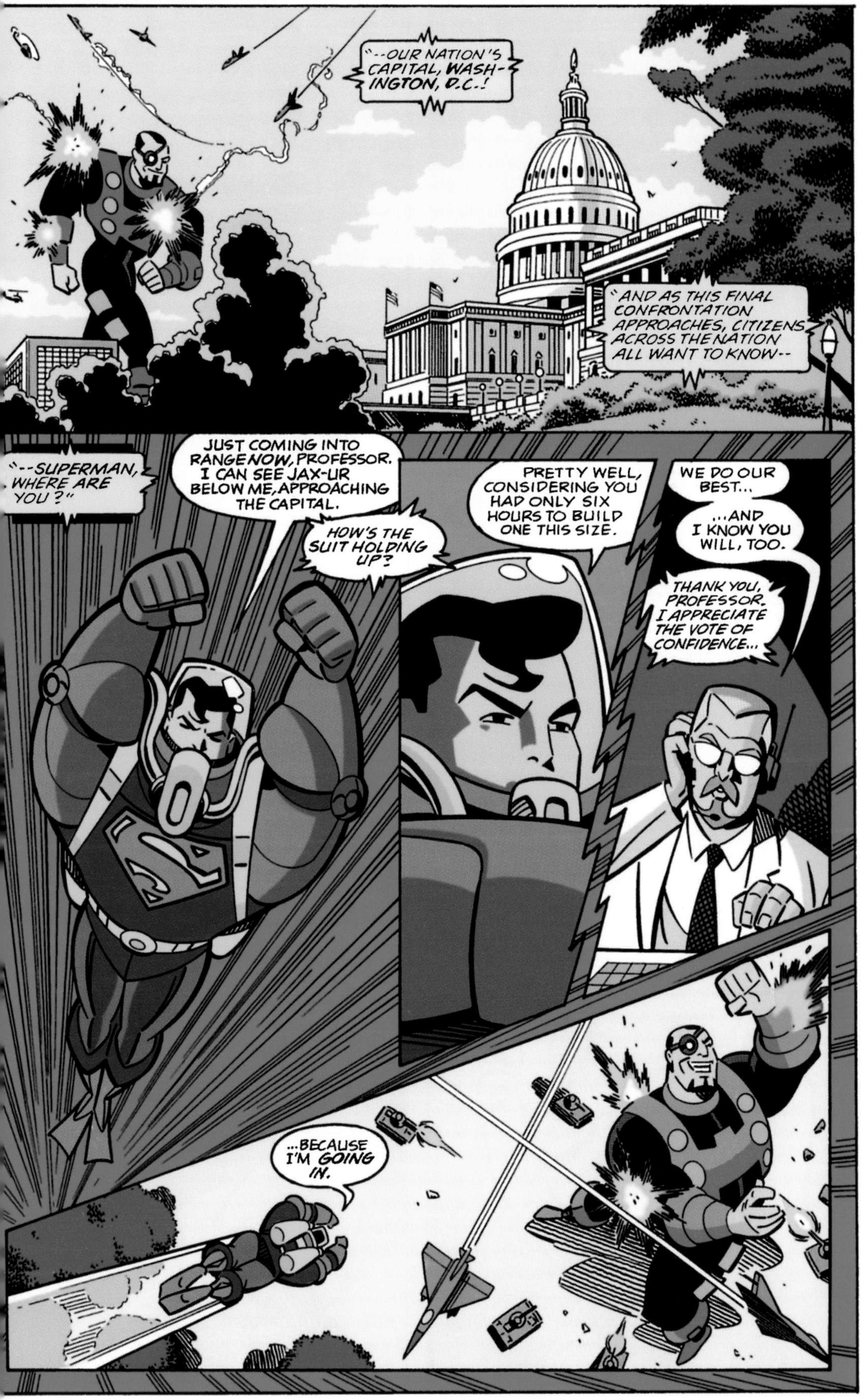
"--OUR NATION'S CAPITAL, WASHINGTON, D.C.!
"AND AS THIS FINAL CONFRONTATION APPROACHES, CITIZENS ACROSS THE NATION ALL WANT TO KNOW--
"--SUPERMAN, WHERE ARE YOU?"
JUST COMING INTO RANGE NOW, PROFESSOR. I CAN SEE JAX-UR BELOW ME, APPROACHING THE CAPITAL.
HOW'S THE SUIT HOLDING UP?
PRETTY WELL, CONSIDERING YOU HAD ONLY SIX HOURS TO BUILD ONE THIS SIZE.
WE DO OUR BEST...
...AND I KNOW YOU WILL, TOO.
THANK YOU, PROFESSOR. I APPRECIATE THE VOTE OF CONFIDENCE...
...BECAUSE I'M GOING IN.

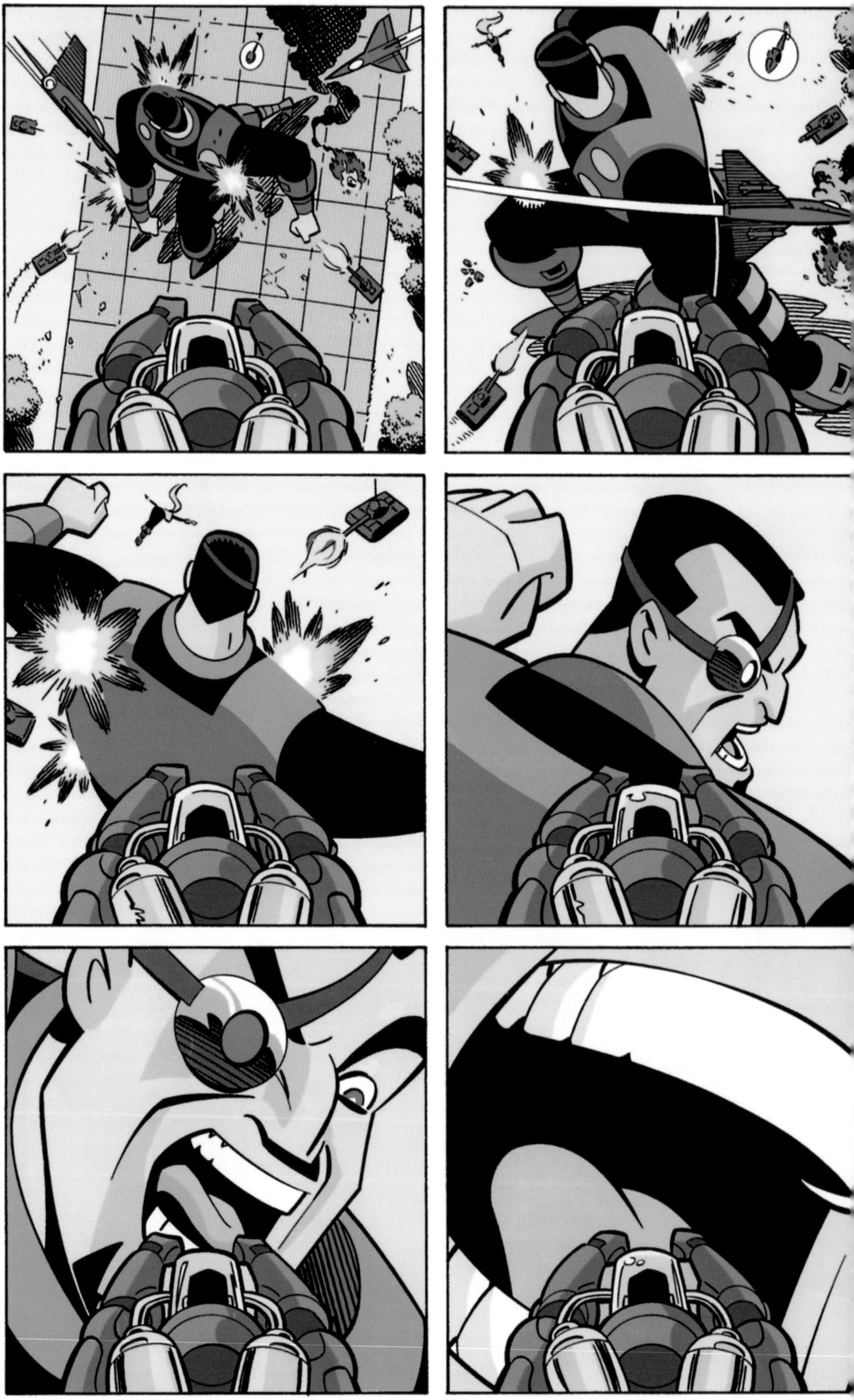

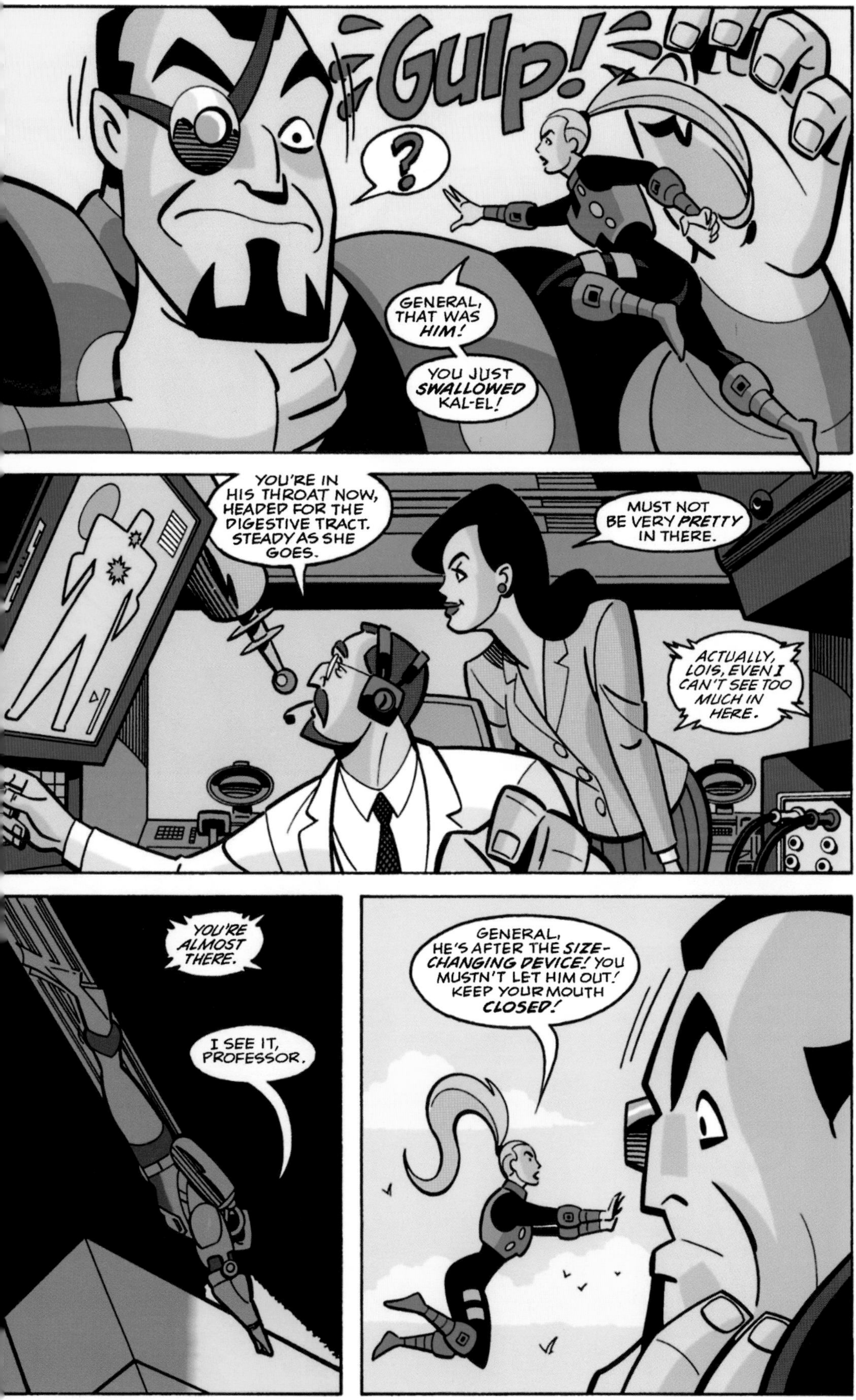
GULP!
?
GENERAL, THAT WAS HIM!
YOU JUST SWALLOWED KAL-EL!
YOU'RE IN HIS THROAT NOW, HEADED FOR THE DIGESTIVE TRACT. STEADY AS SHE GOES.
MUST NOT BE VERY PRETTY IN THERE.
ACTUALLY, LOIS, EVEN I CAN'T SEE TOO MUCH IN HERE.
YOU'RE ALMOST THERE.
I SEE IT, PROFESSOR.
GENERAL, HE'S AFTER THE SIZE-CHANGING DEVICE! YOU MUSTN'T LET HIM OUT! KEEP YOUR MOUTH CLOSED!

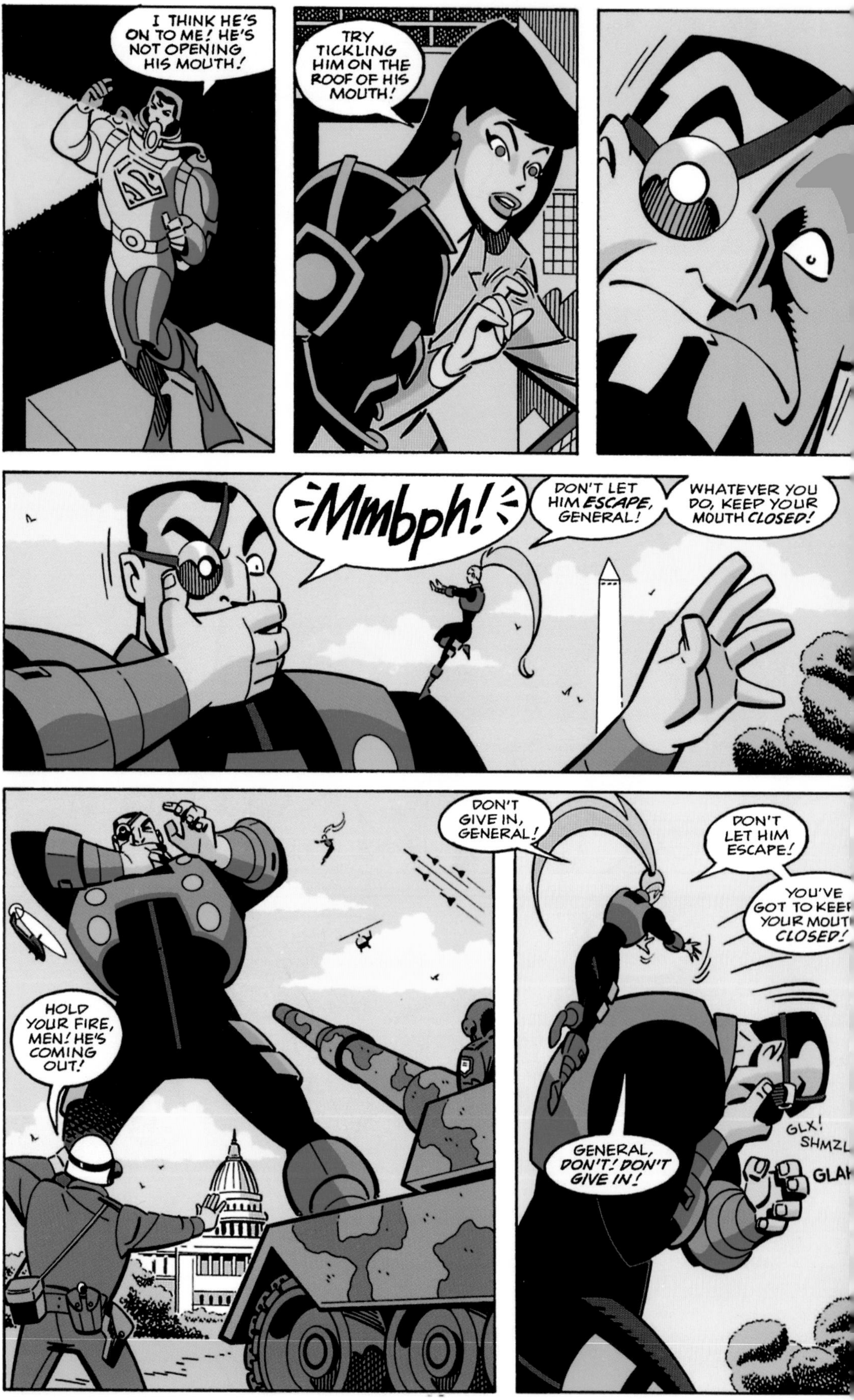

I THINK HE'S ON TO ME! HE'S NOT OPENING HIS MOUTH!
TRY TICKLING HIM ON THE ROOF OF HIS MOUTH!
Mmbph!
DON'T LET HIM ESCAPE, GENERAL!
WHATEVER YOU DO, KEEP YOUR MOUTH CLOSED!
HOLD YOUR FIRE, MEN! HE'S COMING OUT!
DON'T GIVE IN, GENERAL!
DON'T LET HIM ESCAPE!
YOU'VE GOT TO KEEP YOUR MOUTH CLOSED!
GENERAL, DON'T! DON'T GIVE IN!
GLX! SHMZL

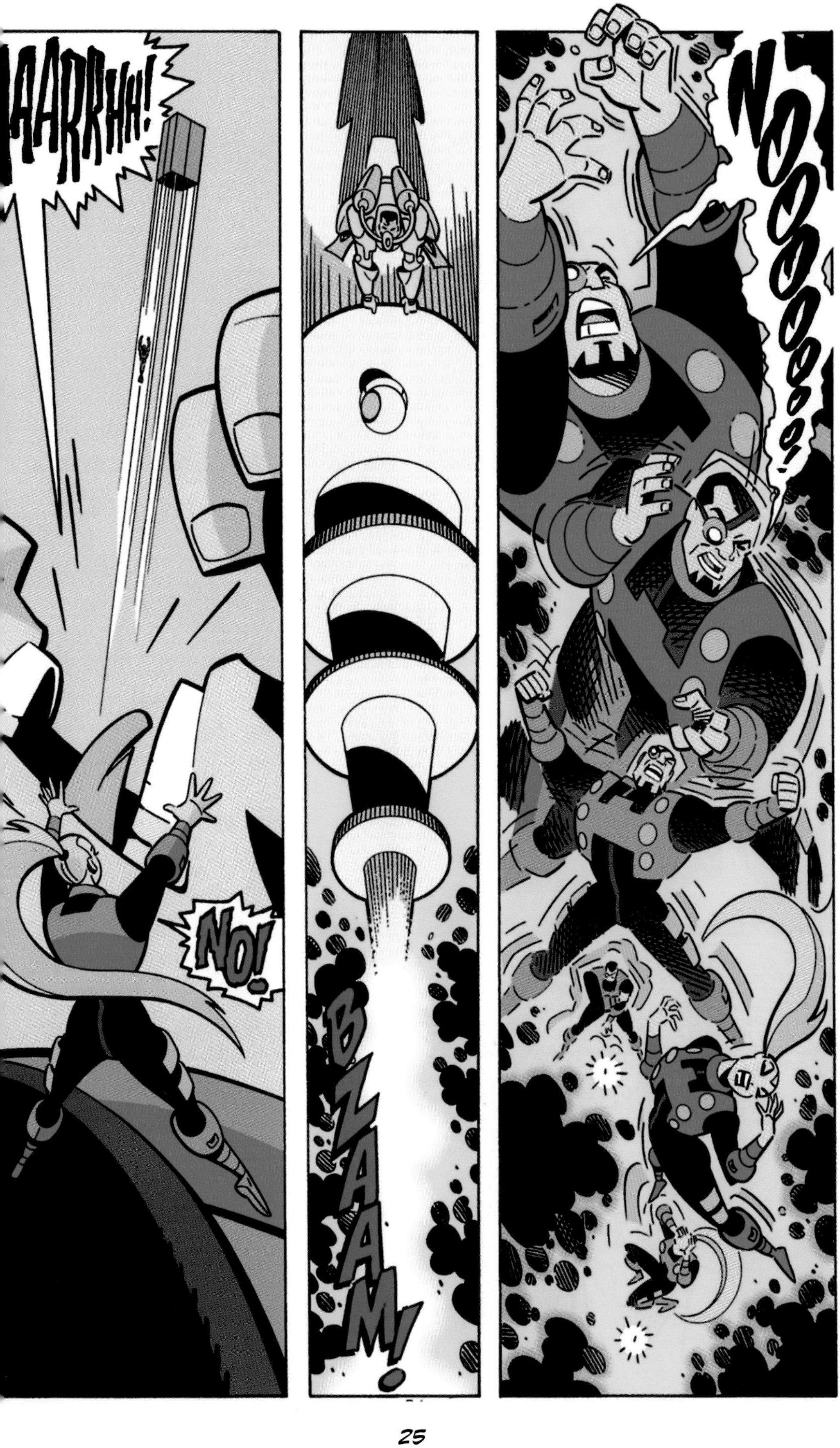
AARRHH!
NO!
BZZAAM!
NOOOOOOOO!

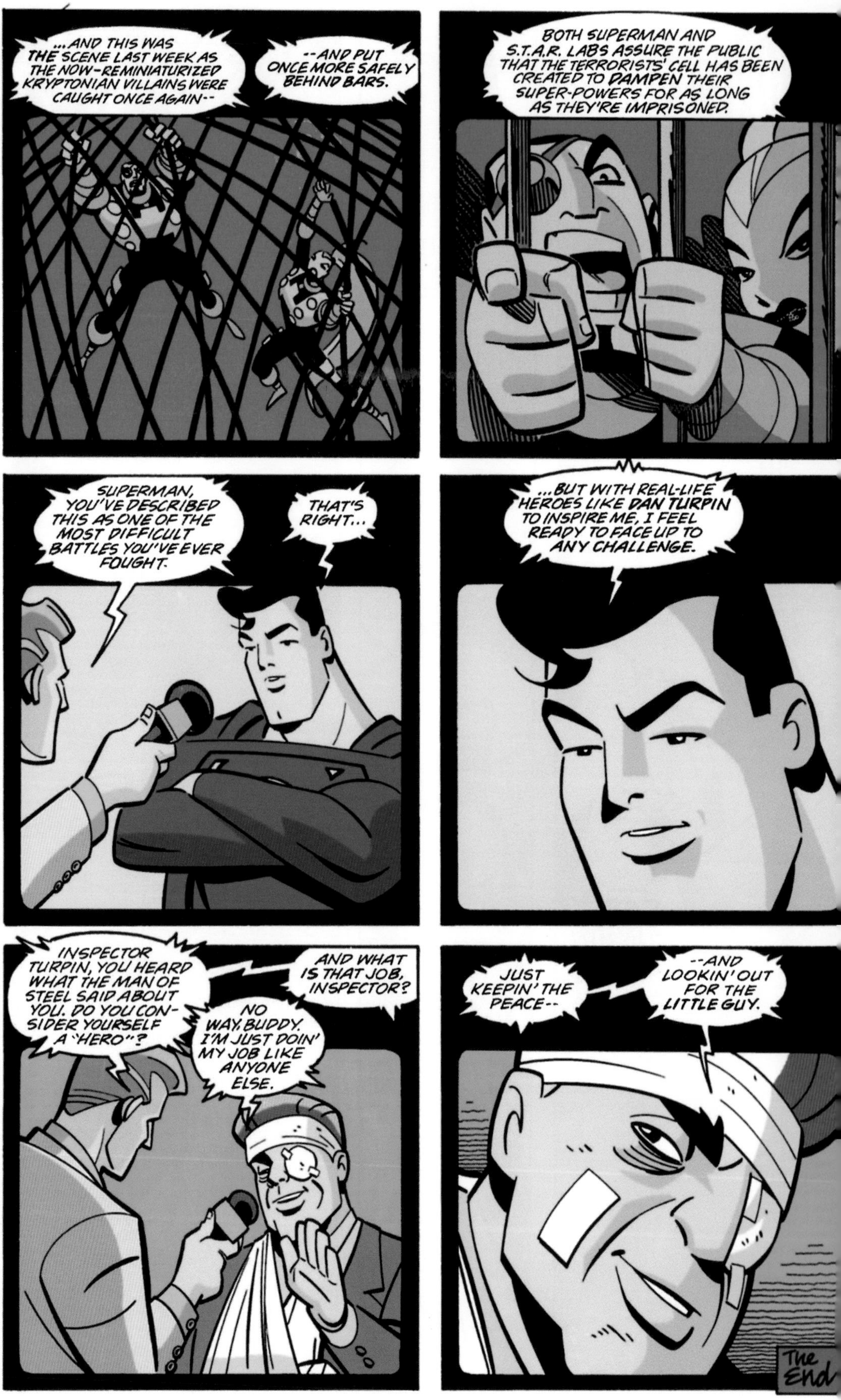
...AND THIS WAS THE SCENE LAST WEEK AS THE NOW-REMINIATURIZED KRYPTONIAN VILLAINS WERE CAUGHT ONCE AGAIN--
--AND PUT ONCE MORE SAFELY BEHIND BARS.
BOTH SUPERMAN AND S.T.A.R. LABS ASSURE THE PUBLIC THAT THE TERRORISTS' CELL HAS BEEN CREATED TO DAMPEN THEIR SUPER-POWERS FOR AS LONG AS THEY'RE IMPRISONED.
SUPERMAN, YOU'VE DESCRIBED THIS AS ONE OF THE MOST DIFFICULT BATTLES YOU'VE EVER FOUGHT.
THAT'S RIGHT...
...BUT WITH REAL-LIFE HEROES LIKE DAN TURPIN TO INSPIRE ME, I FEEL READY TO FACE UP TO ANY CHALLENGE.
INSPECTOR TURPIN, YOU HEARD WHAT THE MAN OF STEEL SAID ABOUT YOU. DO YOU CONSIDER YOURSELF A "HERO"?
NO WAY, BUDDY. I'M JUST DOIN' MY JOB LIKE ANYONE ELSE.
AND WHAT IS THAT JOB, INSPECTOR?
JUST KEEPIN' THE PEACE--
--AND LOOKIN' OUT FOR THE LITTLE GUY.
The End

CREATORS

SCOTT McCLOUD WRITER

Scott McCloud is an acclaimed comics creator and author whose best-known work is the graphic novel *Understanding Comics*. His work also includes the science-fiction adventure series *Zot!*, a 12-issue run of *Superman Adventures*, and much more. Scott is the creator of the "24 Hour Comic," and frequently lectures on comics theory.

RICK BURCHETT PENCILLER

Rick Burchett has worked as a comics artist for more than 25 years. He has received the comics industry's Eisner Award three times, Spain's Haxtur Award, and he has been nominated for England's Eagle Award. Rick lives with his wife and two sons near St. Louis, Missouri.

TERRY AUSTIN INKER

Throughout his career, inker Terry Austin has received dozens of awards for his work on high-profile comics for DC Comics and Marvel, such as *The Uncanny X-Men*, *Doctor Strange*, *Justice League America*, *Green Lantern*, and *Superman Adventures.* He lives near Poughkeepsie, New York.

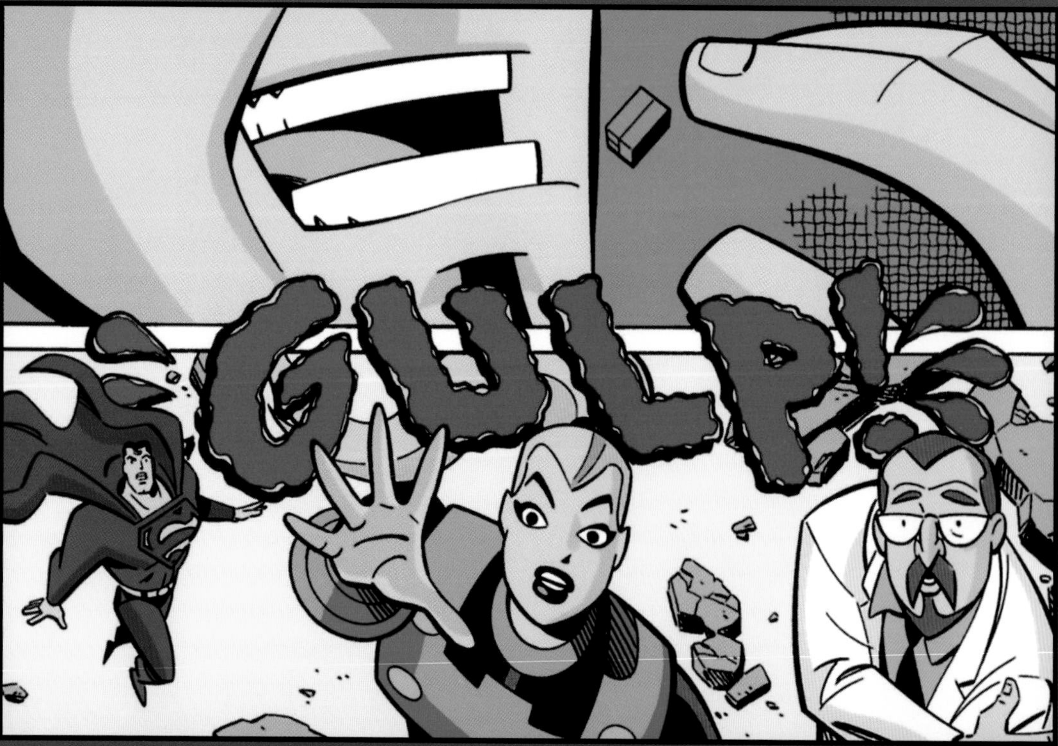
GULP!

accomplice (uh-KOM-pliss)--someone who helps another person commit a crime

complicated (KOM-pli-kay-tid)--something that is complicated contains lots of different parts or ideas which makes it difficult to understand

confrontation (kon-fruhn-TAY-shuhn)--open conflict between two or more sides

conquer (KONG-kur)--to defeat and take control of an enemy

din (DIN)--a great deal of noise

dominion (duh-MIN-yuhn)--power to rule over something

faint (FAYNT)--dizzy and weak

intact (in-TAKT)--complete, or not broken or harmed

presumed (pri-ZOOMD)--thought that something was true without being certain or having all the facts

psychopath (SYE-kuh-path)--someone who is mentally unbalanced, especially a person who is violent or dangerous

restore (ri-STOR)--return to an original condition

stubborn (STUHB-urn)--not willing to give in or change, or set on having your way

SUPERMAN GLOSSARY

Intergang: an organized gang of criminals. They are armed with weapons supplied by the evil New Gods from the planet Apokolips. Their advanced weaponry makes them a threat to anyone, even the Man of Steel.

Jax Ur: an evil general from Krypton. Jax Ur is like Superman in that he receives superpowers from the yellow rays of the Earth's sun.

Krypton: the planet where Superman was born. Brainiac destroyed Krypton shortly after Superman's parents sent him on his way to Earth.

Lois Lane: like Clark Kent, Lois is a reporter at the Daily Planet newspaper. She is also one of Clark's best friends.

Mala: a Kryptonian, like Superman and Jax Ur, Mala is given superpowers by the rays of Earth's yellow sun. She and Jax Ur were imprisoned in the Phantom Zone by Superman after they tried to destroy Metropolis.

Phantom Zone: an inter-dimensional prison for superpowered criminals. Those inside the Phantom Zone do not age, and cannot interact with anyone outside it.

Professor Hamilton: a brilliant inventor and scientist from S.T.A.R. Labs.

S.T.A.R. Labs: a research center in Metropolis, where scientists make high-tech tools and devices for Superman and other heroes.

VISUAL QUESTIONS & PROMPTS

1. What is happening to Jax Ur in this panel? Could the artists have chosen to show the transformation in several panels instead? What would you have done if you were the artist? Why?

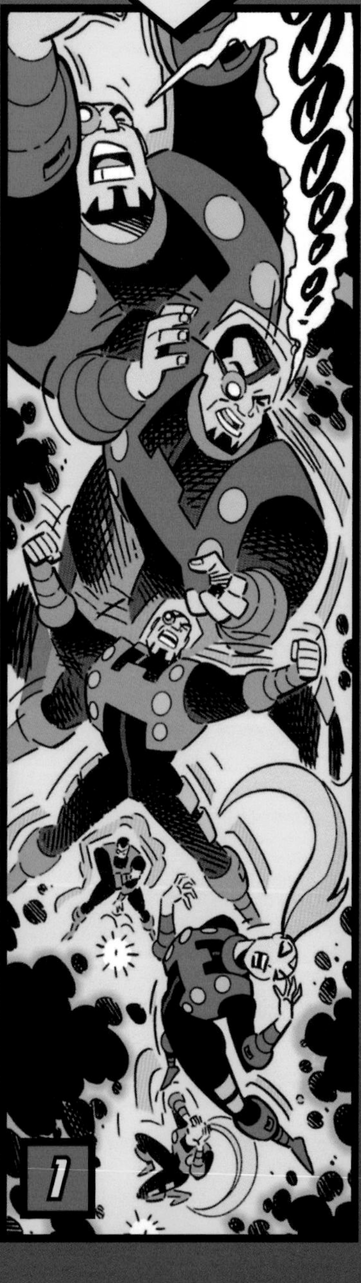
1

2. Why do you think the artists chose to zoom in close on Lois's eyeball in the second panel? Re-read the surrounding panels, then explain your answer.

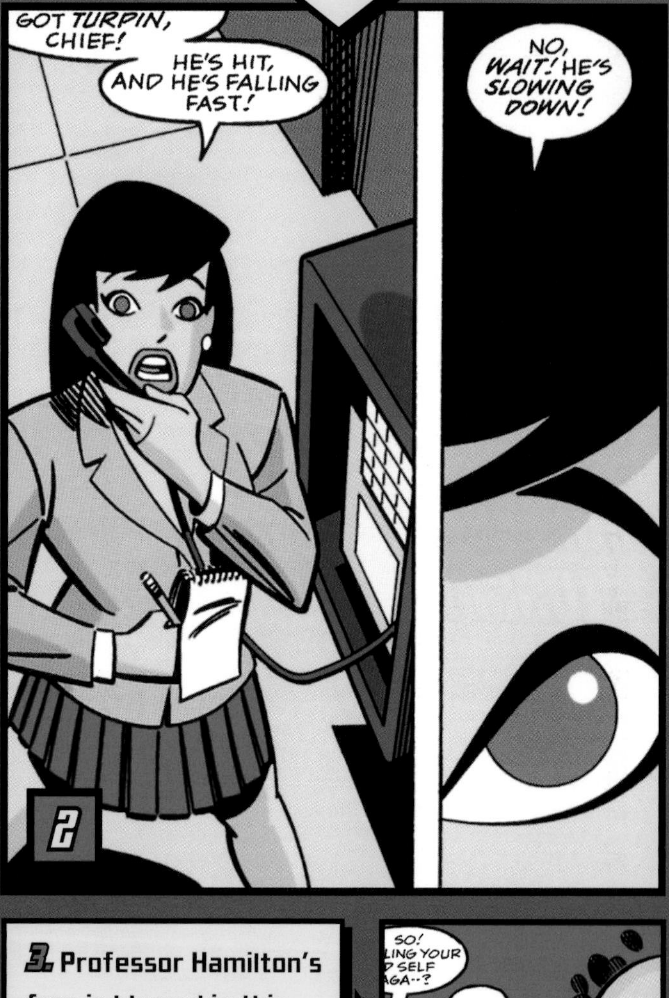
GOT TURPIN, CHIEF!
HE'S HIT, AND HE'S FALLING FAST!
NO, WAIT! HE'S SLOWING DOWN!
2

3. Professor Hamilton's face is blurred in this panel. Why do you think the artists chose to show him this way?

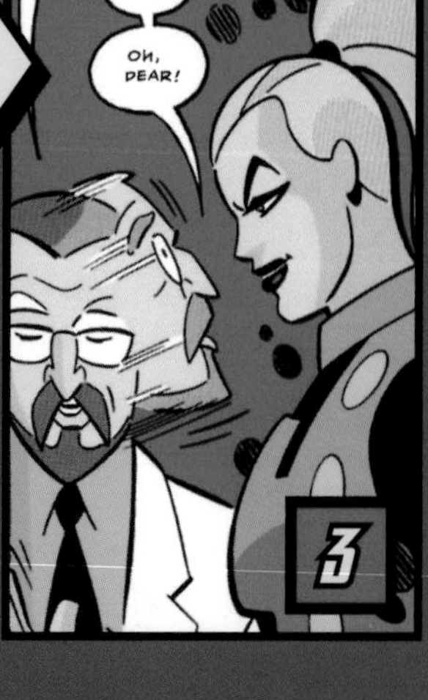
--oh!
OH, DEAR!
3

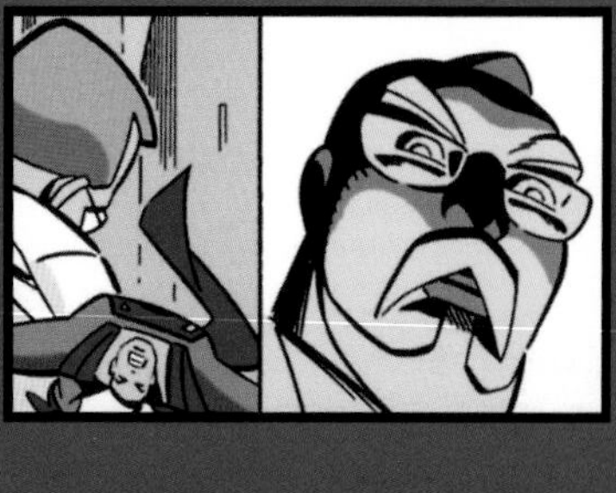

4. This sequence of four panels shows Superman flying toward Jax Ur from Superman's perspective. Why do you think the artists chose to show it from Superman's perspective and not Jax ur's perspective?

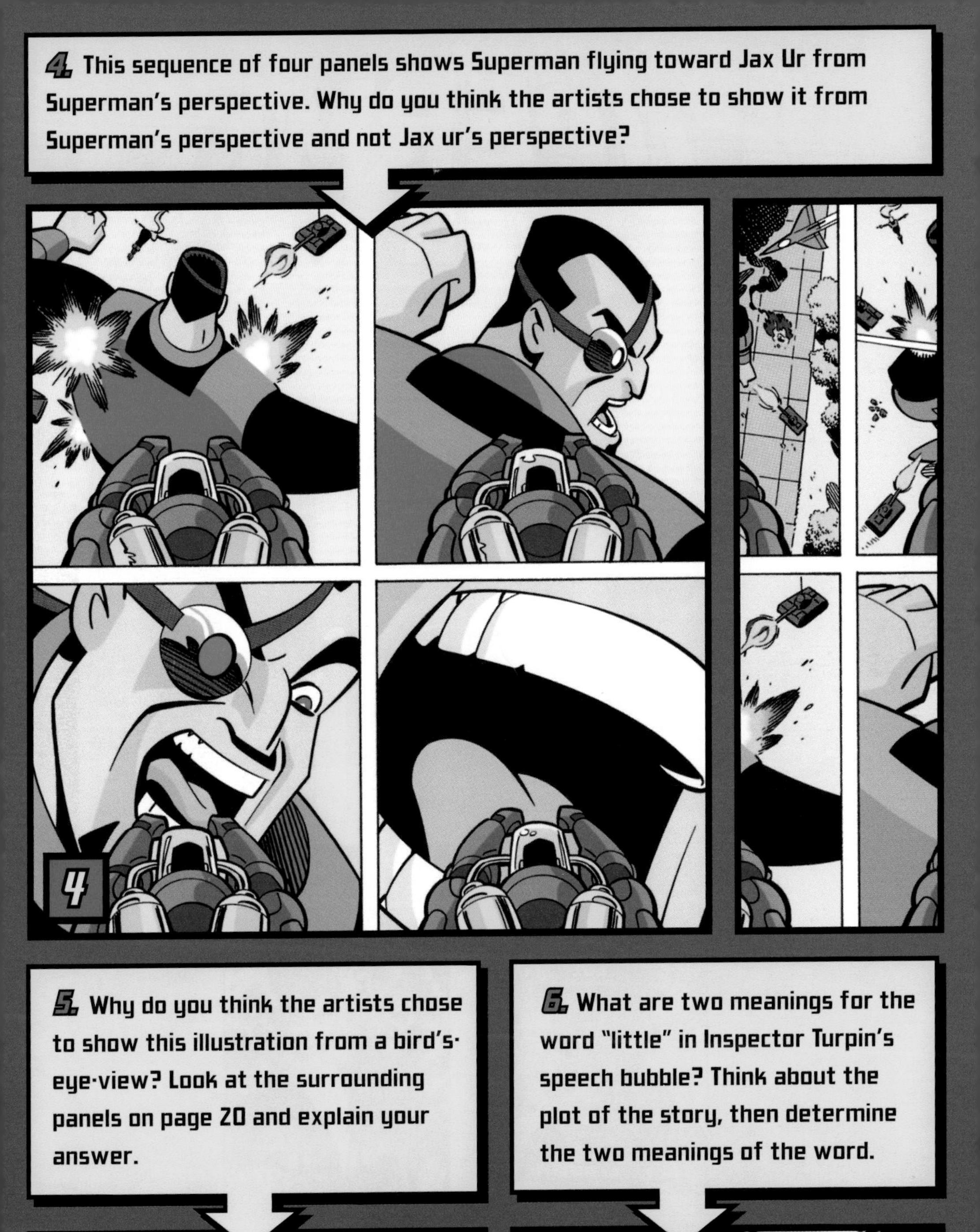
4

5. Why do you think the artists chose to show this illustration from a bird's-eye-view? Look at the surrounding panels on page 20 and explain your answer.

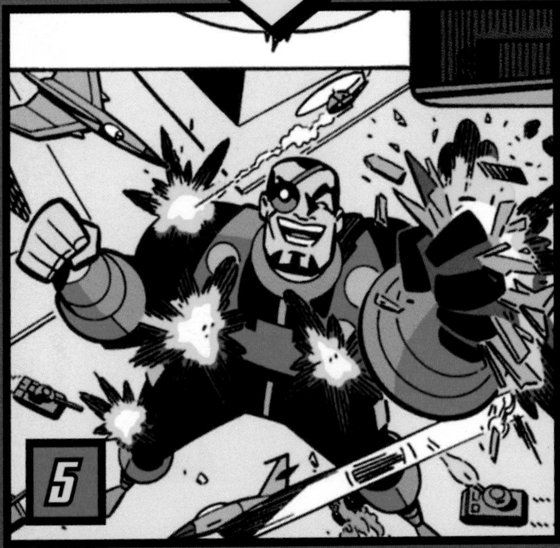
5

6. What are two meanings for the word "little" in Inspector Turpin's speech bubble? Think about the plot of the story, then determine the two meanings of the word.

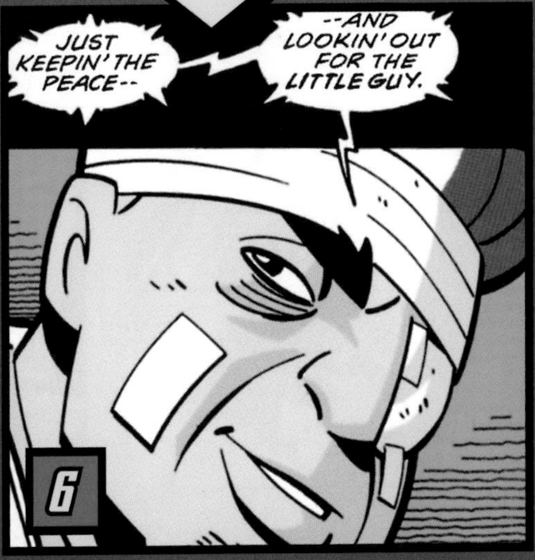
JUST KEEPIN' THE PEACE--
--AND LOOKIN' OUT FOR THE LITTLE GUY.
6

SUPERMAN ADVENTURES

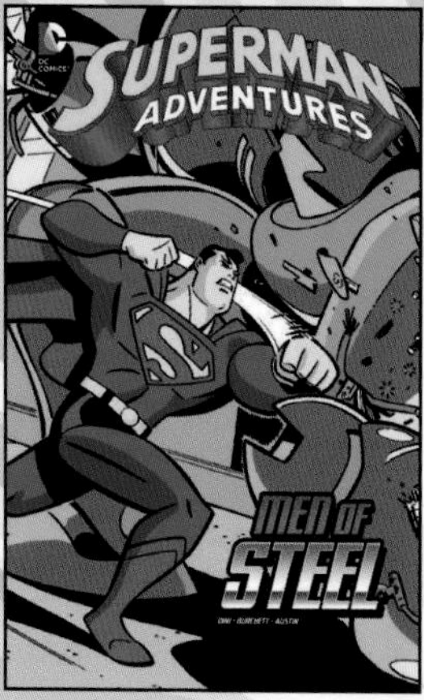

SUPERMAN ADVENTURES
MEN OF STEEL

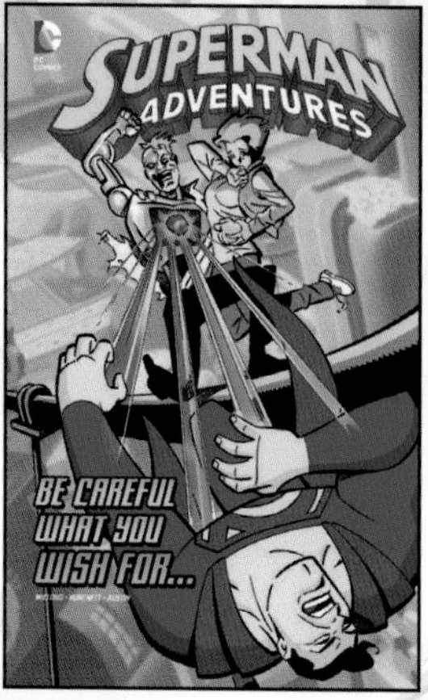

SUPERMAN ADVENTURES
BE CAREFUL WHAT YOU WISH FOR...

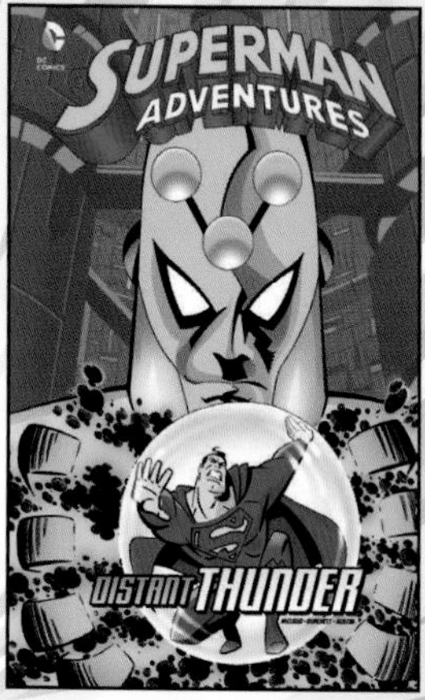

SUPERMAN ADVENTURES
DISTANT THUNDER

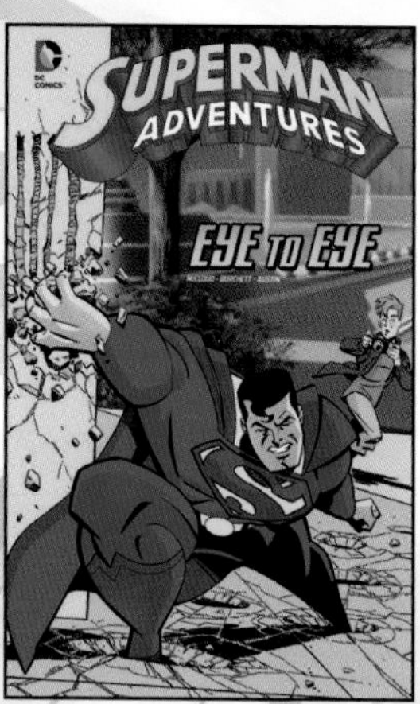

SUPERMAN ADVENTURES
EYE TO EYE

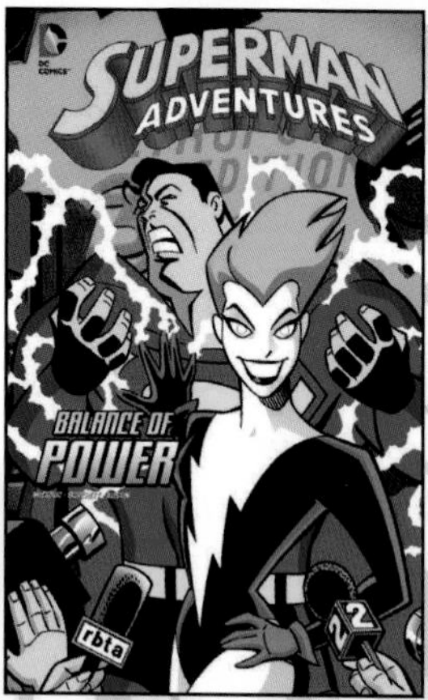

SUPERMAN ADVENTURES
BALANCE OF POWER

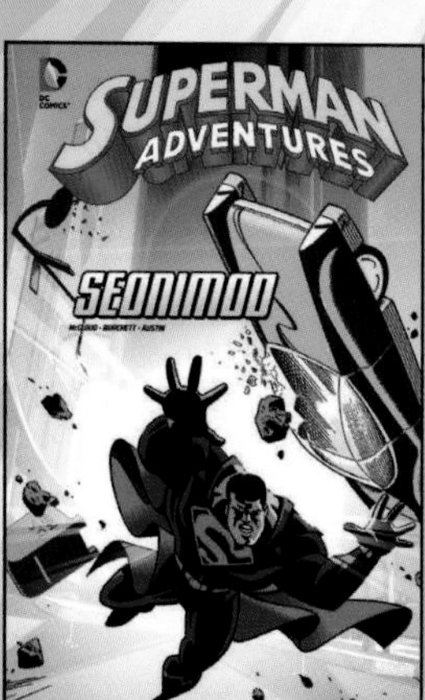

SUPERMAN ADVENTURES
SEONIMOD

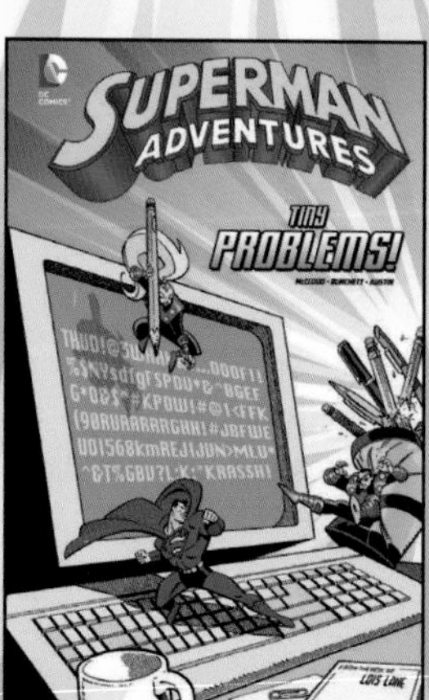

SUPERMAN ADVENTURES
TINY PROBLEMS!

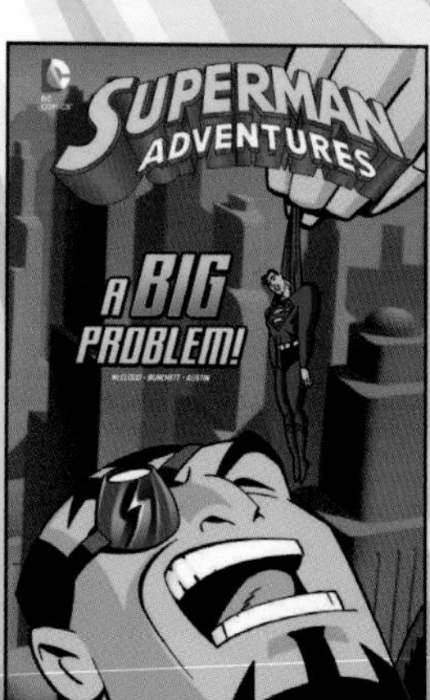

SUPERMAN ADVENTURES
A BIG PROBLEM!

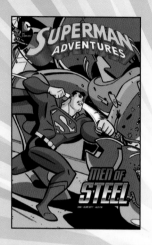